ALWAYS ELSPETH

JOANNE AUSTEN BROWN

ALWAYS ELSPETH
JOANNE AUSTEN BROWN

Book 2 ~ Always Series

Title: Always Elspeth

Copyright © 2021 Joanne Austen Brown

BOOKS BY JOANNE AUSTEN BROWN

Always Louisa ~ Book One: Always Series

Rachael's Jaunt ~ Book One: Come With Me

I want to dedicate this work to my editor Nas and my designer Danielle. You are both two very talented ladies and I am so glad we can work together. You help make me shine.

1

THE PORTREE LOCH — ISLE OF SKYE

August 1818

This was a wonderful spot to watch her before their arrival. The bay was peaceful. The sun had just set, and a silver glow radiated from Suidh Fhinn (Fingal's Seat) behind the manor house. They were five days early, but it did not matter. His aim was to be here. To watch her and hopefully renew the friendship. Maybe also the love they had once had. She would not appreciate his re-entry into her life, but he needed to convince her that this outpost was not a place she could call home and she would waste away here. She had rejected him once, when they were eighteen, but he was determined she would not do it again.

The bay was actually, a loch. He had been to this loch before many years ago but had never seen it so still. Nothing moved around him. No waves. The loch was still and looked like glass. The greying darkness reflected from the loch. He huddled in his coat as the still cool air seeped into his bones. A few lights flickered on the isle but apart from them, the place was desolate. Why on earth had she come here? It would appear she was determined to get as far away from society as she could. He shook his head. She had achieved that goal.

Returning his attention to the house on the hill, he saw the lights of the downstairs rooms go out. Soon there were two lights from the upper floors that he could determine. One to the left. A big room and he could see her uncle moving around it. His curtains were open. Then the subtle light from the top of the tower. Those curtains were closed. He knew she would be there. That was like her. Keep herself hidden. Rise to the highest point of the land and watch everything around her. But do not let them know she was watching. Fingal's Seat was taller than the house, but that tower was the highest of the man-made structures in the area. She was there. He chuckled. Perhaps they should have called Fingal's Seat— Elspeth's Seat. He could imagine her sitting atop the mount, looking down on all her subjects. And some time in the future he would join her surveying her kingdom, wherever it might be.

He turned and went to his cabin. Tonight, he would dream of their reunion.

2

VIEWFIELD HOUSE — PORTREE, ISLE OF SKYE

August 1818

"I want to thank you again Uncle, for your kindness." Elspeth leaned back in her chair and gave a sigh. The dinner they had eaten was beautiful. The cook was only part time, but she enjoyed the times Mrs McDougal was here to feed them. A hunting lodge did not have permanent staff. Except this lodge. They had her. She had arrived two months ago. She came to an almost empty house. Only a part time cleaner and Gilly had been here to greet her. Her uncle had arrived three weeks ago, bringing a boat load of furniture and provisions.

"We are family, and your mother would have wanted me to do something for you. It is not what I wanted but I understand why you are insisting. And please call me Charles and not Uncle. Uncle sounds so old."

She chuckled. "Yes, Charles. But I want to earn my keep. I appreciate the fact you took me in when no one else in the extended family wanted to know I was alive. So, by being your chatelaine here on Skye, I can still have a good life and help you, in return for your kindness."

"This can be a temporary situation you know. The ton would forget..."

"I don't think so, Charles. After what Freddie has done, I will never be acceptable in their sights ever again. And frankly, I am not sure I ever want to go back. It is too..."

"Painful. Sorry my girl, I understand."

She watched his eyes, and she could see his pain. He knew what she felt like, but she did not want him bringing up any bad memories for himself. Losing his sister—her mother—was a blow to him, beyond words. They had been so close. She watched him shake his head and then he continued.

"Well, you will always have a home here and at my estate. I will see to that. You have done so much to ready the house for the hunt, I can tell you. Now let us discuss the hunters arriving next week, shall we?"

"Of course." She reached into the pocket of her dress and pulled out a folded sheet of paper and a small stumpy pencil and placed them on the table in front of her.

"Prepared I see, as usual. Lord Godfrey and his sons Edward and Thomas. The two younger men can share the back, double rooms. Lord Farraday and his secretary Mr Arthur Thomas. They can have the two side rooms in the old wing. His Lordship will be happy in the larger room, of course."

"Of course, but Charles, just give me the names and I will be sure they get the right room as per their station. I have to do my job after all."

"Very well, Elspeth." He paused and then handed her a sheet of paper from which he had been reading. "All the names are here and how many servants are coming as well. I will leave them in your capable hands." He stood and headed to the door. "By the way, join me in a while for a cup of tea before you retire. And we will confirm all the details." He left the room.

She looked down at the sheet. Lord Farraday. Her lips curved in a smile. It would be wonderful to see him again. He travelled everywhere with his secretary now as his arm never quite recovered from his accident.

"Sir Chester McIntyre and his son Oliver, Lord Broderick and son George, can it be…James Raeburn, my James Quinn Raeburn. Lord Donald Raeburn and his sons, James and Lucas. I believe so. Oh, Uncle, no wonder you want to discuss this group over a cup of tea."

If it were James, the James whose heart she had broken and who had broken her heart…she would be staying well and truly in the background. She did not need to be reminded of love.

The darkness was complete. She adored the tower at night. Her uncle had insisted that the tower was for her. It was his private quarters, but he had made it clear when she moved in that this was the best accommodation, and it was for her.

She stood at the open window watching the moon rising and glistening on the loch beneath her. It was the only light spreading across the loch that stretched out beneath her. She often woke at night and would stand looking out over the waters. Being on the non-business side of the small fishing village of Portree, she often did not see any movement other than the waves or a storm. Tonight, she had woken from another bad dream. The reoccurring dream of her brother killing himself. She had not actually seen it happen but her dearest friend Louisa had. She had wished she could take that image from her friend. And over this last year she believed she had. It always seemed so real to her.

Standing at the window at this time of night, looking at the bay was her lot. A sigh left her lips as she scanned the loch for movement. She preferred the Scottish word loch over bay. It seemed so much more romantic as a loch. Was that a lamp light? She looked and watched the light vanish. It was there and then it was not. She looked again but the light did not reappear. She continued to scan for it but it didn't reappear. She must have imagined it.

It was then that a small rowboat appeared on the still waters. And a dull and subtle light came from it. She watched it as it glided towards the peninsular on her left. It had come from the anchored ship. The only ship in the harbour. She had watched it come in late that afternoon. There were the occasional ships that would seek out the Portree Loch to rest before they made their way around the peninsular, known as the Lump to the Portree harbour.

She went to her telescope. This had been one of the treasures from her home at Broadbend that she had not sold. So much of the family jewels, property and paintings had to be sold to pay off her father's and Freddie's gambling debts. It had been her father's and one of the magical instruments that had made her childhood so special. She had been determined to keep it. She needed to remember her father as the man he was when she was a child. What he had become was too painful to remember. As was her image of Freddie.

She directed the scope towards the boat. Two men rowing and two men seated at the rear. She wondered why they were out and about at this hour. She watched as they pulled up on the little beach near smugglers cave. A chuckle left her lips.

They must be smugglers.

But then her chuckles stopped abruptly. They each lifted a small crate from the boat and carried them into the darkness of the cave. All eight boxes were taken into the hideout. What were they hiding?

She closed the curtain and carefully touched her way to her bedside table where she lit a candle. She noted the time and what she had seen, writing them into her journal. She used pencil again preferring the instrument to the ink she used for her letters. Her journal was her friend. Here she could write her thoughts down as if she were writing to Louisa or Chalanor. Often, she would share her experiences directly from the journal when she wrote to her dearest friends. She blew out the candle, felt her way back to the window and opened the curtains again. The rowboat was gone and only the white tips of the small waves beyond the loch, showed any movement.

The moon had risen higher and it was then she noticed there were two ships in the harbour. Another must have come in under the cover of darkness. But which? They were closer together than was usual.

Unusual.

But from which one had the little rowboat emerged? The moonlight had provided her with more information than she was comfortable with. She shook her head and made her way carefully to her bed and crawled in. She was tired.

Go to sleep.

Your answers will come tomorrow.

3

SILVER LIGHT

The silver light of dawn stretched out over the loch. She stood again in front of the window. In the light of day, it was clear there were two ships. She had seen correctly. The way they were anchored made it hard to distinguish the two as separate vessels.

She turned and finished applying the cap to her head. She hated it but it helped to make her invisible when the aristocracy were around. Her hair was one of her crowning glories, as her friend Louisa had always said. She remembered the day Louisa and Chalanor had their church wedding. She had little blue forget-me-nots pinned into the curls of her dark chestnut coloured hair. She poked a loose curl in under the cap. Those days were gone.

Word had come before they retired last evening that guests had arrived early. Her uncle had not said who but she had most of the rooms ready. She would be sure to find out who had arrived so she could allocate them to the correct room. But which ship are they on? After all, one of the ships had harboured the smugglers she had seen. What if she had imagined the rowing party? And was she about to face a new villain? She had enough of villains. She wanted a peaceful life.

Making her way down the stairs, she came to stand with her uncle who was awaiting her.

"I am sorry about this but the letter that accompanied the announcement of guests arriving was marked urgent. I wanted to find out what was going on before I let you know."

"No need to apologise, Charles. This is your home. You can do as you please."

"Elspeth, it is our home." He gave her his usual 'don't say that again' look and continued. "The Raeburn's have arrived early. Lord Raeburn has some political matters to discuss with me. His sons are with him. But I will arrange for my Gilly to take them out hunting and touring the island. You will not need to entertain them."

She lowered her head and hoped her uncle would not see the blush she knew was spreading across her face. Her cheeks were burning.

"They are adults. I am sure they can manage. So do not fret." He placed his hand on her shoulder and then placed it by his side again.

She kept her head bowed.

"It would seem, that I owe you another apology. The date for their visit was arranged before you accepted my hospitality."

"I am your chatelaine. There is no need to explain."

He stood taller than he had before. "You are my family, and I am proud of you. I would not want you to feel uncomfortable. I remember what James meant to you."

He paused and she looked into his eyes. He knew how she felt. He continued.

"But they have also brought a guest with them. Someone you know."

"Someone I know? But I know very few people in Scotland."

"It is Lord Farraday's daughter, Delia."

"Truly? How wonderful. It will be a delight to make her acquaintance again."

"I hoped you would say so. She is to be reunited with Lord Farraday here. I was sure you would not mind. And that you might appreciate the company of another young lady, instead of having to deal with all the men who will be here."

"Oh, Charles I am delighted, and I know that Lord Farraday will be also. I promise to spend as much time as I can with her. I want to find out about where she has been. So, I can write to Chalanor and ease his mind."

"I am very proud of you, my dear. Thank you. I am sure she will be happy to spend time with you also."

He turned on his toes and headed down the stairs.

He was so dear to her. A more thoughtful uncle she could not ask for. He was the only person who had cared about what happened to her. And she was family as he constantly reminded her. Her mother would be so proud of her brother if she could see the way he looked after her. She headed down the stairs after him and thanked God that she had such a wonderful friend and uncle.

She entered the breakfast room and sat opposite him.

"It would seem it is I who needs to apologise, Charles. I do not want to presume too much. I feel I am an embarrassment to you. What Freddie did is unforgivable…"

"But, dear girl, it was his downfall, not yours." He lifted his hand to silence her. And yes, she was about to correct him. "You have taken on his sin as your own and I do not like it. In fact, I hope that while you stay with me, I can convince you that others do not see you in the light that you have placed on yourself. It is not right. You are innocent and I wish to show you that. It is your brother that people need to condemn, not you. And you need to stop condemning yourself. As I said, I am proud of you. Many women could not have been as brave as you, under similar circumstances."

She slowly got to her feet. Warm tears flowed down her cheeks. She went to her uncle, leaned down, and hugged him.

"Thank you, Charles really. Thank you."

He leaned into her hug and returned the embrace. "Your mother, my dearest sister, was an angel and you are part of her. An angel in your own right. Now sit down and have your breakfast. We have things to get ready."

She returned to her seat and they had a pleasant meal together. She assured her uncle that all would be ready for the guests' arrival and that tea would be provided in the evening room when they arrived.

She was determined to do all she could to make this time a joyous one for her uncle. His kindness…overwhelmed her.

4

JAMES

There was a path from the loch up to the house. She watched as men carried luggage up the hill. All were isle men and servants she assumed of the Raeburns. After the coming and goings, she finally noticed the three tall gentlemen making their way from the loch. All well dressed and out of place on this island path. And with them was Delia. She was taller than she remembered. Her mother had been very tall. She was wearing a hat and a cloak. Elspeth looked forward to greeting her.

Descending from her tower she went and stood with her uncle in the foyer of the new section of the house. She loved this area as it was a big space and her tower sat right above it. It was only a few years since her uncle had it completed. The original house was large by isle standards but was old and needed to be refurbished. So, he undertook to make a manor house out of it. And he had, adding extra rooms, large lounge areas and a dining room that was larger than most. The wood-stained features made her feel she was in a manor house in London and not on an isle off the west coast of Scotland.

She checked her skirts were in good condition.

"You look wonderful, my dear. Though I wish you would not wear that silly cap. After all, you are my niece. Promise me no more cap."

His stern look gave her no option but to agree. She nodded.

"Good. Now let me see you smile. Here come the Raeburns."

First was Lord Donald Raeburn. She had met him some years ago. He looked the same but with more grey at his temples. She curtsied but kept her eyes looking down at his boots.

"Charles, how wonderful to see you."

"Raeburn, my pleasure."

"And we must thank you for your kind invitation. It is good to leave Edinburgh behind us for a while. And Miss Ismay, it is a delight to know that you will be here this visit. My sons require civility, and I am sure your presence will provide it. I have also brought a guest, Lord Farraday will desire to meet again."

He stood before her and bowed. She lifted her eyes to see both joy and happiness in his lordship's demeanour. Something she had not seen in the aristocracy for some time.

"It is my pleasure to see you again, sir."

"Please call me Raeburn. Everyone does."

Then James was standing in front of her. Her breath caught. He was more handsome than she remembered. Probably because he was a man and not an eighteen-year-old who thought himself a man. But she was drawn to him which she had not expected. After all these years?

His dark red, yes, chestnut hair, like hers, was curling around his collar. He was tall, well over six feet. Taller than the last time she had seen him. His attire was that of a gentleman, despite being in the outer parts of Britain. And his eyes were as blue and deep as the seas around the isle. Blue grey and mysterious.

"It is indeed a pleasure to see you again, Miss Ismay." He took her hand and bowed to her. "A great pleasure."

Lucas gave his brother a little shove. "Actually Miss Ismay, the pleasure is all ours. We have been talking of nothing else since we heard that you would be here. You are looking very well. It is so good to see you again."

She chuckled. "Hello Lucas, if you don't mind me saying, you haven't changed at all." She noted James still held her hand. And it seemed he was unlikely to let go.

"Have I not grown? I know that I am a good inch taller than my brother. And I was a much shorter person the last time we met."

"That is very true, Lucas, sir..." And it was. He was taller and thinner. Still growing. Handsome, but James outdid him in looks.

"Please call me Lucas, you always did."

She sensed the eyes of James, always on her as before. It would seem, that had not changed either. And he still held her hand. She gently pulled her hand away from his hold.

Delia now stood in front of her.

"My dear Delia, I am so glad to see you again. It has been so long. I do hope you are in good spirits." They curtsied to each other.

"Dear Elspeth. When I heard that you were to be here my heart sang. I have so much I would like to talk to you about. Especially how my dear brother Chalanor and his lovely wife Louisa are doing."

"I will be delighted to share my correspondence and stories with you. I am also delighted that you will be reunited with your dear father. A finer man you will not know."

Delia lowered her head, and Elspeth could see the blush rise to her cheeks. She looked up and smiled at her and she knew the coming weeks would be a wonderful time of reconnection for her and Lord Farraday. Elspeth turned to the gentlemen who waited patiently for them to finish their greeting.

"Please gentlemen, let me escort you to your rooms to freshen up."

She was glad her uncle had spoken. Somewhat rattled, she let out a breath she had been holding. Having James by her side again and knowing Delia would be returning to the bosom of her family, was a dream. But it was reality, and it began to excite her. These were good things, and she could do with some good experiences in her life.

"I will have tea brought into the evening room uncle, for when you are ready."

"I do hope you will be joining us, Miss Ismay?" James was staring at her, waiting for a reply. And her uncle quickly made things very clear.

"Of course, she will, gentlemen. And please call her Elspeth, after all you are old friends."

She stared at her uncle and he smiled at her. She had not expected an invitation. She curtsied and made her way to the bell and gave it a pull.

As the gentlemen made their way up the stairs, Morag the only maid, came to stand with her.

"Can you bring the tea into the evening room in ten minutes, Morag? But please will you first escort Miss Delia to the room on the first floor next to my tower stairs?"

"Yes ma'am" she curtsied and turned towards the stairs. "They are handsome gentlemen."

"Yes, and gentlemen is what you should remember." She had said the words more harshly than she intended.

"Yes ma'am" she replied and went on her way. Elspeth noted the rise of colour on her cheeks.

She looked at the stairs as Morag escorted Miss Delia to her room. Morag would be the death of her. She observed too much and did not mind saying so. Being a maid was her part time occupation. She also worked down at the beaches harvesting seaweed. But even that job was in the decline. She was a good girl, just not used to having to wait on ladies or gentlemen.

She made her way to the evening room and checked the fire was burning well. August was cool but some of the days were still warm. She again chuckled. Four seasons in one day was the Isle of Skye. A fire was always welcome.

All she could see was the smiling face of James. And the touch of his hand. And that fragrance. Yes, all three men smelled distinctly of sandalwood. She took a deep breath in.

Stop it. Don't think about him.

Her heart it would seem was no longer frozen but was thawing out near the warm fire. And perhaps it was the fact James was here.

———

James entered the small room at the rear of the building. It was comfortable and clean. Not what he was used to but for such a far-flung place it was more than acceptable. He could see Elspeth's touch. His bags and trunk were at the foot of the bed and their valet would no doubt unpack them after he had dealt with his father's belongings.

He went and stood at the window and looked out over the stable yard. Two of the servants were wandering around. It was no use. He could not get the image of Elspeth out of his head. That stupid silly cap. He hoped he could talk her out of wearing it. Her auburn curls were poking out from underneath, no doubt trying to escape. His lips curved in a smile. She was still as beautiful as she had always been. Now even more so.

"She still is as beautiful as ever." Said his brother as he came through the doorway.

"Still don't know how to knock I see..." he turned to face him. He looked like the cat that had caught a mouse. "Yes, she is."

"Perhaps she might be interested in a young buck rather than an old rake."

"Dearest brother, I am no longer a rake, as you well know. I have every intention of settling down. And my intention is to settle down with the love of my life, not your imagined love."

His brother came and placed his hand on his shoulder. "You need not worry little brother, oh I mean big brother, she is yours and I am aware of it. But it is so very nice to feast one's eyes…"

"Just so long as you remember you look and do not touch. And you are only an inch taller, so please do not call me your little brother."

"Yes sir. Do you think she might listen to you? I do hope so. It would be grand to have her as a sister. But she has matured and may not be interested in being your love."

"I hope she can see she need not hide away in the west. It was her brother who was the villain. She needs to stop thinking she is tainted by him. She is herself. And I hope I may renew a spark that had once existed."

His brother went to the bed and sat down. "Some people don't see it that way. Oliver McIntyre and George Broderick for example."

He came over to stand before him. "I know. So now that we have arrived before them, we can try to convince her that she is safe with us. And will then avoid those clods. If they treat her badly, I do not know what I would do. But I want her to trust us."

Lucas nodded and he hoped he would help him to convince her she was safe with him again in her life. He also hoped he could convince her of much more.

Their valet knocked on the open door and excused himself as he came in and started to unpack his luggage.

"Lucas, hurry and freshen up and we will see if we can beat father down to tea."

He smiled as his brother turned and dashed out the door to ready himself. He took a deep breath.

Ahhh.

The faint smell of forget-me-nots. Elspeth. She was everywhere in this house.

5

COMFORT

Morag carried the tray of cups and saucers into the evening room. She placed them on the table and returned to the kitchen. Elspeth placed the cups and saucers out around the table and removed the tray. Morag returned and placed the tea pot on the candle burner sitting in the centre of the table. She took the tray from Elspeth.

"I will return with some items to eat and milk and sugar, ma'am."

"Thank you, Morag."

Morag curtsied and smiled and then left the room.

Her uncle came in and sat in one of the voluptuous sofas. Although old pieces, she had the cushion parts restuffed but had kept the original silk Damask that was still in good condition. She had spent many days cleaning them. They were not very fashionable anymore, but they were practical for light entertaining.

"This chair has never felt so good to sit in since you had the cushions plumped up. Thank you. It has made them very comfortable even in an old hunting lodge."

"It is still your home away from Edinburgh and your estate and needs to be serviceable. I have just made adjustments."

"And I love them, my dear. You can alter whatever you want. I also hope you do not mind that I bought some of the pieces from Broadbend. I just did not wish to see them disappear forever. Your mother will be glad they are here."

"It really does help to make things feel like home. Thank you, uncle. Especially the pieces from my original bedroom. Mother would be pleased."

Morag re-entered and placed the last few things on the table. She curtsied to them both and again, left.

"Would you like tea, uncle?"

"Yes, my dear. Black please."

She poured him a cup and was placing it in her uncle's hand as Lucas and James entered the room.

"You called this the evening room, did you not Elspeth?"

"I did Lucas, but it really is an all-day room. We have morning and afternoon teas in here and have our evenings here after dinner. It is a very versatile room. After all this is not a great manor house. It is a hunting lodge."

James was standing at the window looking towards the loch. "There are some trees to give you privacy. Yet the outlook is beautiful."

"You get better views from the rooms upstairs. Your father has one of the best aspects." Her uncle had responded to James as she was unsure if the comment was even directed to her.

Thank you, Uncle.

But she was left in no doubt about the next question.

"Do you like it here?" He turned and was looking at her. His eyes were penetrating. Her stomach gave a little flip.

"Yes, I do. It suits my needs, and it is quiet." She dropped her gaze and turned back to the teapot on the table. "Can I pour you some tea, James?"

He came and stood next to her. "Yes, milk and no sugar. Thank you." She poured him a cup and handed it to him. Their hands touched and suddenly she was back in London remembering the last time she had given him a cup of tea. She pulled her hand away and picked up her cup and went to sit next to her uncle.

She sat quietly with her head down and drank her tea. Her emotions could not be trusted. She did not want to look at him for fear of revealing her feelings.

He had not wanted to make her uncomfortable, but it would appear he had. She had answered his question but immediately had become sullen. Why had he done that? He should take care when speaking to her. He should not make her uncomfortable. He quietly looked at her as she seated herself next to her uncle. His brother looked at him and shook his head. Confirmation he had gone too far. He sat in the seat opposite her and Charles.

"Charles, I must say that you have done a lot to the house. The extension is quite dramatic."

Charles looked at him with kindness. "The house is much larger than your last visit here. I do believe that was ten years ago?"

"That's right and I believe the extensions were started not long after that visit."

He enjoyed reminiscing about his last visit

"We McDonalds love our great houses. Though I would hardly call this a great house."

I believe your cousin has built a new Castle in Armidale."

"It is a grand house, but it looks more English than Scottish. Which is such a shame as a Scot designed it. James Graham."

James detected an increase in the Scottish accent as he continued to talk.

Through the whole conversation, Elspeth said nothing and kept her head down. This was not the Elspeth he had known all his life. She was so cut off, timid.

"I do not wish to be rude, but I cannot stay silent any longer."

Just then, his father entered the room with Delia on his arm.

"I hope that you have said nothing amiss, James?" He asked.

"Not yet father. But we have been conversing a great deal about life here on the isle and Elspeth has said nothing. Elspeth, please talk to us. Are we not old friends?"

She looked solemnly at him. "I do beg your pardon sir, but I have been sitting quietly listening to your conversation." It was said with no emotion.

"That's my point. When have you not joined in the conversations of others? This is not the Elspeth I know."

She stood and her uncle grabbed her hand. "Please sit, my dear. I do believe that someone is concerned for you." She did but it appeared reluctantly.

"I am. Please explain to me why you have retreated to this isle?" He turned to Charles. "I am sorry sir, but I do not wish to offend."

"No offence taken, my boy. Go on."

Elspeth stood and looked down at her uncle.

"I am a servant here, not free to discuss my life. I am no longer part of society. This is my private life and I have no intention of having it discussed with strangers."

She turned and left the room.

"I am not a stranger Elspeth…please." he called after her.

She did not return.

"That did not go well." Lucas surmised.

"Really? Do you think I couldn't determine that for myself?"

"I only meant…" But James would not let him finish.

"Delia, is she the same?"

"No James, she is not. But she has been through a great trial as I have. Am I the same?"

"She is not Elspeth. For heaven's sake, how has she come to this?"

Charles stood and came to stand before James. "I will but say one thing, James. Her heart is crushed. What her brother has done she cannot forgive and blames herself. She thinks she has no worth. And you heard her, 'she is but a servant'. Which she is not but I can't get her to see reason." Charles was looking earnestly at him. He realised that Charles not only agreed with him but was pleased he had spoken up.

"But that is ridiculous. It is Freddie's actions people condemn. Certainly not her. What can we do?"

Charles placed a hand on his shoulder. "I am counting on you, boy, to help me convince her. Unfortunately, society in London gave her condemnation. She has not gotten over that. She is quiet because she can trust no one..." He raised his hand to silence him. "You must be gentle and give her time. Show her she is still the same to you."

Charles left the room, abandoning him and the others to discuss the future, no doubt of them all. He had overreacted. This was ridiculous. And he might have ruined his chances.

"Elspeth, please wait for me." Her uncle called to her. She was walking down the path to the beach. She stopped and turned to wait for her uncle to catch up. "They are merely concerned for you, my dear."

"I know, I just feel so uncomfortable with the members of the ton."

"But my dear, these men have been close friends of yours and your family. You can't condemn them especially as they do not condemn you."

"I have not seen James Raeburn in ten years. How can he sit

there and tell me I am not behaving like myself? How on earth would he know? I am not a young girl anymore. I have changed." She said those words with a great deal more force than she had intended.

Charles smiled. "Perhaps he had hoped you had not changed much. But I understand. Ten years can change a person. But your silence is a dramatic change in your persona. You would have to agree."

"Oh Charles. Ten years and a brother who committed murder and then killed himself. Common knowledge for all members of the ton, yet he has the nerve to think I am still the eighteen-year-old girl he once knew." She turned and continued the walk down the path and she heard her uncle's steps as he followed.

"Perhaps you could see it from his perspective for a moment."

She stopped walking and turned to face him. She folded her arms.

"And what perspective do you speak of?"

"He might still care for you and observes the pain you are in. Believe me it is obvious to anyone who knows you."

"Oh uncle, I'm not in pain. And why does he have the right to assume I am? I am happy here because I want to be. I am a little out of sorts at the moment, because I had not expected to see James or his family. And Delia. People from my past life."

Her face was warm and despite what she had said she knew her uncle was right. She was in pain. A pain of change, loss, and guilt she could not seem to erase.

"Possibly, but the fact he is concerned, must suggest he may still hold a part of his heart for you. That he might know you still? And what your brother has done does not change his feelings for you or who you are."

She turned and continued down the path. This time she could not hear her uncle follow. He called out, "He just might, you know."

But she did not want to listen to his side of the argument. She came to the beach and went over to her left and found her favourite rock. She sat down and took a deep breath. Turning to look up the hill, she saw her uncle was returning to the house.

This was difficult and complicated.

But her uncle could not see it. She had enjoyed her time here on Skye and did not want to be driven away by men who think they can rule her life or tell her how she should feel or how she should behave. She never let any man do that before and she was hardly going to let anyone start now. It was not going to happen. Even if part of her heart, set aside just for James, was rejoicing at his return.

She looked out over the loch and examined that part of her heart she had ignored for ten years. She needed to take the time. And in front of this loch was as good a place to start as any.

---

*H*e greeted Charles as he came to the top of the path.

"She is stubborn, my boy. I know your intentions are in the right place, but she will not hear of it. Leave her to her thoughts. She will return by luncheon and I am sure you can tell her you are sorry for your words."

"But I am not. She is not happy and anyone who knows her can see it."

Charles placed his hand on his arm. "Offer her friendship, my boy. The rest might follow if you are prepared to wait. She is hurt."

James looked down at the lonely figure on the beach. He would apologise and then offer friendship. He sat on the bench under the tree and waited for her to return to the house. He could kick himself. He had badly judged his comments. It was obvious the real Elspeth was just below her shallow mask. She was there. He would find her. And if only she would allow him to take the mask away forever, he would do so.

———

*D*ong. Went the luncheon gong and she made her way back up the path to the house. As she reached the top, James stepped out to greet her.

His words came out in a rush. "Elspeth, please allow me to beg your forgiveness. I had no intention in upsetting you. I apologise if my words were not acceptable. I want us to be friends again. Please forgive me."

She looked into his pleading eyes and could see his sincerity. She put out her hand readying herself for a handshake. He slowly took her hand.

"I would appreciate your friendship and thank you for your apology."

She removed her hand and passing him, headed for the house.

———

"*T*hank you." He said as she went by. He placed his hands behind his back and looked out over the loch. Perhaps his bad start at renewing their friendship had been repaired. He would need to be attentive to her and not overreact again. He had few more moments of contemplation, thinking of a possible future together, then turned and followed her in.

———

*F*rom the ship he had no idea what had happened but had watched her sitting on the beach for some time.

Finally, she went back to the house. He saw that James Raeburn greeted her and they seemed to shake hands. Strange.

Had she been watching the ship? Had she suspicions of the activities they were involved in?

No, he concluded. There was more going on and he could not detect. After all, none of them even knew he was here. He would keep watching. His plans were heading in the right direction.

6

OLD PASTIMES

The conversations over luncheon were amicable. None of the tension from earlier was present. His apology had lessened her temper.

"Tell me, my dear," Lord Raeburn continued, "What aspect of this quiet life do you appreciate the most?"

It was a genuine question from his lordship, and she was pleased to answer. Because there was no judgement from him. She looked at James and then back to his lordship.

"I would have to say the quiet, sir. I love to walk in the gardens and the forests. I enjoy the walk to the village and greatly appreciate the varied climate."

"An honest answer, my dear. But you have yet to face a winter here."

"It is true." She emphasised. "However, I have inside pursuits. I love to read and Uncle Charles' library here is very good."

"And getting better Elspeth as I have ordered some new material for you."

"That is very kind of you, Charles. I look forward to seeing what arrives."

"What of your passion for painting?" Delia asked her.

She smiled at her but then looked at James who appeared to be hesitant.

Elspeth wanted to put him at ease. She had overreacted to his penetrating questions this morning. God. She was so wound-up and tense. Delia knew of her love for painting. She would answer honestly. It might put his mind to rest.

"The last year has occupied a great deal of my time in dealing with the estate of my parents and brother. To be able to do what one wants to do and not what has to be done has been a blessing. This is the first guests we have had since I arrived. So, I could paint a few scenes from the island."

"I would be happy to see them if you have the mind to share." Delia looked at James.

"As would I." he added.

"Perhaps one of our evenings I can bring them down and you can give me your honest opinion of them."

James smiled at her as did the other guests. Perhaps the coming weeks would not be so hard after all. And she would appreciate the time with those who would not judge her too harshly. James had not meant to judge her. He was concerned for her. It was clear now.

Her uncle added his piece to the conversation.

"Perhaps, if you are interested, we can tour some of Skye's historic landmarks and the hunting. Elspeth has been reading a great deal about the local history, haven't you, my dear?"

"It is true, Uncle. I must admit I was surprised at just how many special things have occurred on this isle. I would be happy to share. But for now, I need to arrange for further jobs to be completed before we have more visitors. I will see you all late in the day." She stood, curtsied, and left the room.

*J*ames stood and excused himself and followed her out.

"Miss Ismay, Elspeth, if I may. Can I ask if I could have a private word with you later today?"

"Certainly, James. Shall I see you in the garden in say two hours? The garden on the new side of the house."

"Thank you. I will see you then."

He stood there a moment and watched her walk away. She held herself tall and straight. As she always had.

Oh, if only things would be right with them now. He would make amends.

"She will be fine now." Charles said as he came to stand next to him.

"Thank you, Charles. Whatever you said, her anger has left her."

"You need to allow her to talk when she is ready. Do not push her. It was a full week after I had returned, before we were able to discuss Freddie and the events which brought her to me. And I have seen her many times before and since his death. Give her time."

"I will. Thank you again."

"I'm counting on you to help me, James. She knows I am encouraging you, but she has no idea I asked you to come after I had determined she planned to live here for good. I too want her to return to society. Even if she never goes back to London, I hope she can become part of the Scottish society. I believe they will treat her better."

James watched Charles go to the stairs and head up.

Oh God, he was still in love with Elspeth. He always had been but coming here and seeing her again had brought new life to him. Maybe he could now convince her of his true feelings. Ten years had not dulled his longing. His heart still thudded, and an unexplained power went through him every time he saw her.

*A*fter confirming with the cook and Morag all was in order, for the rest of the day, she retired to her room for some peace and quiet. She had promised to talk with James this afternoon. Probably, he wanted to make amends for his outburst that morning. She was not her usual vivacious self. She shook her head. Would that part of her personality ever return?

She had discussed it with Louisa at length in their many letters. Louisa had encouraged her to tell her everything. She would do what she could to support her. Her heart lightened, Louisa and Chalanor were her two strong stable pillars. Apart from her uncle, they were the only true family she had.

James' reactions were understandable. The girl he knew was not the same as the woman who stood before him.

She read through some of her letters and her journal. After a while she went over to the window and looked over the loch. Silver glints shone as the small waves entered the loch. The two ships were still in the bay. Strange. The ship the Raeburns had arrived on, was not leaving until the next day. But ships rarely stayed in the loch for more than a day. Surely the other ship would have gone around to Portree by now? But it had not.

Oh well.

Better jot it down in her journal. Going to the mirror, she removed her cap. She tidied her hair and then went downstairs.

*J*ames was seated at the end of the garden bench as she came around the corner of the house. She walked straight towards him. She knew he still was concerned he had said the wrong things this morning. She wanted to make him relax. He stood and waited for her. My, he was so handsome.

She could not believe how good he looked. He was one of the most handsome men she had ever known and a real gentleman.

Stop. Don't think that.

Again, he took her hand and gave her a bow. "Thank you for agreeing to spend time with me. There were a few things I wished to discuss with you."

"I do hope you have forgiven me for the way I reacted this morning…"

But he stopped her. "Please, it was my fault and I wish to share with you why I was concerned."

She took her hand from his and sat on the bench. "Of course, James. You sound so very serious."

"I am and I guess it is in part because I have been horrified in the way the ton have treated you. You do not deserve the condemnation."

She smiled and lowered her eyes to the ground. Heat of embarrassment rose from her neck to her face.

"I do not say this to embarrass you. I have come on this visit in part to assure you of the Raeburn's friendship and support."

"James, how truly wonderful of you and your family. Thank you."

"But I also come as a warning. There are some who will continue to make your life a scandal. But I want to say, I will not allow that to happen while I am around you. I may not have always been your friend, but I will not allow anyone to treat a lady in a despicable manner."

She looked at him. He looked tense but there seemed to be truth in all he said. He wanted to protect her but from what? If he were telling the truth, she would allow it as she had always trusted him. Despite not wanting to marry him.

"I am far from the society that abandoned me, James. I have no illusion I will ever be acceptable in their eyes. It is in part why I accepted my uncle's offer to come here."

"I understand and appreciate that. But the Scottish society are more, forgiving…no that's the wrong word…"

"Less judgemental?"

"That's the word. They see people as they are and do not judge them on the actions of others. They judge less you might say. You are who you are, and they will see the real you. On that and that alone will they examine you."

"Ahhh. I understand. You and my uncle have been speaking."

"I won't deny it, however before you make any conclusions, I will have you know that he only confirmed what I already knew."

She lifted her head and looked into his eyes. "What did you already know?"

He never let his eyes move and kept them focused on her.

"That you would blame yourself for the actions of your brother." He placed a finger on her lips. "Please do not answer. Think about what I have said and if you believe me to be correct then I wish to discuss more things with you. Let me know this evening and we can arrange to sit here in the garden tomorrow and discuss matters further."

He stood, bowed, looked deeply into her eyes. "I'm glad you got rid of the cap. Your hair is beautiful." He turned and went back towards the house.

She remained seated. She had not expected to hear those words. He had always adored her hair. Seeing the cap would have distracted him. And his comment about her brother? Perhaps after all these years he did know her still. It was true that she could not shake the actions of Freddie and continually looked for ways or times she might have done something to have prevented his hideous crimes. But they never came, and she always blamed herself for not seeing the stress and torment her brother was experiencing. Not seeing anything, which drove her brother to do what he did.

She took some deep breaths and eased herself back on the bench.

He was right and from afar he had known what she would be thinking.

Shocking and surprising.

But that lifted her spirits. Had he really been thinking about her all these years? Perhaps, there were others like her uncle who would not condemn her. She had not expected this and spent a while seated on the bench to take in this revelation. And along with those thoughts, her mind kept drifting back to James. She pictured his smile and her own lips lifted.

She would speak with him again. She wanted to know more and why he would waste his time coming to her, to reveal his thoughts. There was more to this than what she had just heard. She could wait till tonight.

7

NOW, THE TRUTH

They had a relaxing dinner and were in the evening room awaiting the arrival of tea. The gentlemen were enjoying a whisky made at her uncle's estate on the mainland. Made in secret he confessed. To keep the tax collector away. He loved the occasional dram but tonight he had declined this, in favour of tea. Delia sat with her, also drinking tea.

They were chatting about people they both knew and updating each other on events while they had been in different places.

James made his way around her chair to the vacant chair next to her and placed the whisky on the side table between them. He was looking at her. Was he waiting for an answer to what he had proposed that afternoon? She excused herself to Delia. Delia smiled and turned to face away from them.

Elspeth decided to address him first. "James, I must say that I am amazed that you have gone to so much trouble to speak with me. You are right, I do blame myself for not seeing what my brother had been doing."

He smiled, a warm and gentle expression on his face. There was no sign of victory over her. He seemed relieved. She continued.

"I also am surprised that you have even thought of me after all these years."

"I will reveal all but not till tomorrow. We will meet in the garden again. What time do you suggest?"

"After breakfast if you don't mind. Then after our conversation you can walk with me to Portree. I need to pick up some fish for our dinner tomorrow evening."

"Do you not have servants who can do this for you?" He asked.

"I am my uncle's chatelaine. It is part of my duties."

"Ah yes. I would be happy to accompany you."

She smiled as Morag handed her a cup of tea.

"Can I get you one too, sir?" she asked

"No, thank you." He picked up his glass and took a sip of the amber fluid. "I will have this."

He stood. "Until tomorrow. I hope you have a pleasant sleep." He returned to stand near the fire with his brother. She could see his smile on occasions and noted he seemed more relaxed. Things seemed to be going well. Well, but in what way?

She turned to talk to Delia.

"Have you been in contact with your father?" She asked.

"Papa…it is so nice to call him Papa again. Yes, we have been writing to each other. James helped me to get in contact with him. I had hidden myself from them, so well, I knew I would need to give them evidence it was really me."

"I remember when you left, your father and Chalanor spent many months trying to find you."

"Chalanor came very close to finding me at one stage but my great aunt was able to steer him away. I did not want to be found. Please understand? I hated my mother, for telling me Papa was not my real father. I believed my life to be a lie."

"I do understand."

"I knew that you would. I am sorry you have had to face your own demons."

"Thank you. But I will recover, and I believe you have already." She did not want to think about what she had been through so brought the subject back to Delia.

"I am in good spirits. At first, I was shocked to hear what happened to my mother. But can we talk about this later? There is too much to talk about now. But know I have come to terms with the events. I am tired. I will retire shortly."

"Can I suggest that we spend some time tomorrow discussing this more fully? I want to know where you have been and what you have been doing. For now, I suggest we both have an early night. We have very busy days ahead of us. Well, the hunters have." She chuckled.

She stood and then reached down and took one of Delia's hands in hers.

"I am glad you are here, Delia. I really am."

"Thank you, Elspeth. I too am glad to be here and to see you."

She sat on the same garden bench she had found James seated on yesterday. She had many experiences with members of the *ton*. They had all been disastrous. They only wanted to cause her pain and convince those who would listen, she had to have known what her brother was doing.

Could she be happy around the Scottish elite? After all, her mother had come from a well-established Scottish family. Her uncle was still a highly regarded member of that family. He had already been arguing with her, saying she took after her mother. Sweet natured, honourable. And poor Freddie was more of the Ismay line. Cowardly, traitorous and nothing like the MacDonalds. But despite her father's faults, her mother had loved him with all her heart and perhaps had overlooked what may have been in his nature.

All these thoughts disturbed her. How could she remove one part of her family line and maintain the other without it being affected? Could she easily dismiss it? Did she want to?

She was fond of this part of the garden. She had already painted the scene not long after she had arrived. It was always green and lush. She could smell the salt that came off the loch and listened to the distant sounds of the water lapping the shore. It was a place of peace. One she always wanted to have. It was in an unexpected place, but she would take it.

She watched as James and his brother Lucas came towards her. She was about to stand but he signalled her with hand gestures to stay seated. She nodded.

Lucas sat on one side of her and James the other. She suddenly felt small and fragile surrounded by these men and shook the feeling away. She had never ever wanted to feel fragile.

"My dear Elspeth, I hope you don't mind if I attend this little discussion," began Lucas, "But I hope if I can confirm for you what James has to say, you might believe what we wish to tell you is true."

"Well now you have my full attention and perked my interest. Please continue."

James took her by the hand. "I know you think that I have no feelings for you. But I do."

She looked into his blue-grey eyes. He did have feelings for her still. She could see it. But did she wish for that attention?

"I can see you mean what you say James. I know I hurt you all those years ago and I am very sorry I did. But at the time…"

"We were young and did not know what our futures would hold."

She smiled. He was more mature, as was she.

"All I ask," he continued, "Is you listen to what we have to say and perhaps we can come to a better understanding of each other."

"That sounds very wise."

"Father knows what we want to say," Lucas went on. "And he has given us his full support and to you also."

"Then I suggest that we talk about what brought you here so I too can fully understand."

James still had hold of her hand. Now Lucas picked up her other and she was captivated by both their actions.

"It began… No, I will go further back." James pondered for a moment then continued. "When we got news as to what happened to your brother, I became very concerned as to what had happened to you. At first the news was solely on Freddie, but I wrote to a friend and asked if he could find out what had happened to you."

"We were all concerned," added Lucas, "especially when word came your estate was to be sold."

"I appreciate your concern. Thank you." She looked from one gentleman to the other.

"But news came from my friend that you had packed up what you could and was able to keep and would come here to your uncle's hunting lodge and not to his estate. That your uncle had purchased some items from Broadbend to add to the newly modified building here."

"That is all true. Your informer was accurate." She was tempted to ask who had told him but reconsidered and waited to hear what else James had to say. She had to admit his revelations so far surprised her.

"We were glad your uncle had taken you in, as such, because we knew those in London were unable to look at you after what your brother had done."

"That is also true."

"It enraged me. How could they judge you so? You had not done the deed and it was very clear to those who knew you it was beyond anything you would even think about."

She lowered her head and said nothing.

"Word spread through Edinburgh society—as a daughter of a

MacDonald—you would be more than welcome to come home. When it was known you would come to your uncle, many of us were relieved."

Lucas then picked up the story line.

"However, I heard rumours. And then James began to hear them also."

"My goodness you sound so serious. What on earth did you hear?"

Both men gave her hands a squeeze. James continued.

"Some of the elite were saying they should do to you what your brother had done to others."

A chill went through her.

Surely not.

She looked from one gentleman to the other. This is not what she expected but then she really had not known what to expect. This revelation was a shock. How could the elite even think it? A shiver ran up her backbone. Her blood ran cold. Did they really mean that she should be murdered?

"We are sorry to be so blunt," James went on, "But those who were saying it were not only serious but had the means to do so. Hence the reason we have come early, before the rest of the guests. Two of the most vocal men are coming for the hunting party."

"And you are worried that they will be hunting more than deer?"

"Exactly." The men said in unison.

The pause hovered between them and lasted for some time. She was stunned. They watched her, as the information they revealed penetrated her mind. Finally, she could remain quiet no longer.

"What do you suggest I do?"

"You fight it with our help. Forewarned means forearmed."

She looked into James eyes. "You can't expect me to fight them?"

"Not physically but as to their preventing you coming into Scottish society, with our help we can beat them."

"What do you suggest?"

Lucas let go of her hand and James took it into his other hand. She altered her position on the bench so that she was facing him. Lucas stood and moved away slightly.

"Marry me. Our name and position can protect you."

"James…"

"I do not say this lightly. But I wish to protect you."

"But James, what of love? You may want to marry another someday. And I have no intention of getting married ever."

"Please understand, I have loved you even after the day you rejected me. I have no intention of marrying anyone but you."

"But James…"

"I know you think I am saying this to save you only but as Lucas will confirm, my eyes have been for you only, all these years. Being a rake was not what I wanted but suited me, while I was angry with you. But soon, I concluded, I had placed too much pressure on you, and I had waited for the right time to make amends."

"It is true, Elspeth." Added Lucas. She looked at Lucas and could see the truth in his eyes.

"But we have not seen each other in ten years. How could that be?"

"We have friends who have told us how you have been doing. And I have seen you on occasions in London. Though you did not see me."

She stood up.

"Some might think you have been spying on me…"

"Let us reveal what else we know before you answer or question us further."

"No. I need to think for a moment. You were spying on me. How dare you?" She walked away, leaving both men. She crossed the grass and walked back and forward in front of the dining room window.

How could anyone do this to her?

Her hands made fists and she looked down at them. She wanted to hit something and that shocked her as well. She could feel her heart rate rise. Her anger was about to boil over.

She stopped pacing and just stared at the clench fists, her hands. She opened her hands and then closed them into fists again. Then opened them again. This anger would have to stop. It was not her.

James came and stood in front of her. He took her opened hands and looked at her face. Heat rose to her face.

"I will accept your anger if you feel I have spied on you, but I ask you to hear me out first. Sir Chester McIntyre and his son Oliver are coming, are they not?"

She took a deep breath and let it out. "Yes, they are. But I do not know them or have ever met them."

"Yet, Oliver is the ringleader and George Broderick also." Added Lucas who also had come to stand next to her. "Despite you not knowing them."

"I have heard of George but do not know him either. Why would they think this way?"

"I know it seems strange even unthinkable, but there are some who believe the sins of the brother must taint the blood of the sister. I will not deny it. They are cruel young men. They believe the Scots must remain unblemished by any other nation. And who do they despise most of all? The English man, and you are half English."

She looked up into his grey blue eyes, eyes fixed on her own eyes. She was only part Scottish. It was true. Her father was English.

"But I am innocent. It was my brother's sin."

"I know you are innocent. And I am delighted to hear you say it. I know your nature; you are not the person they describe. They think you are your brother. You are not."

"This is unbelievable. Do they honestly believe I could do what my brother did?"

"Yes, because they do not know you. So, let me make the following suggestion. If you do not believe us and want to see for yourself how they treat you when they arrive, then do so. But as a safety measure, we would like you to consider a temporary arrangement."

"And what is that?"

"You allow us to get engaged so I can protect you."

"An engagement?"

"A temporary one so we can protect you." Lucas added. "If they know you have our protection they will back down. We have strength they will not challenge. If they treat you with respect, then you can ignore what we have said and back away from the engagement."

She started to pace back and forth again. "Are you sure they are involved in this nonsense?"

James took her hand. "Yes. We have no doubt, and we believe they accepted the invitation after they knew you had come here two months ago."

His hand was warm. He again took her other hand.

"And you say you really care for me still?" She looked at his hands holding hers.

"Yes, and I always will. I want you to know that my love for you is real."

She lifted his hand closer to her face and placed it on her cheek. His warmth on her skin expressed to her he was telling the truth. Slowly his other arm drew her into an embrace.

"I need to tell you something." She was gazing into his eyes. "Lucas?"

"Yes Elspeth?"

"Can you go inside and have my uncle and your father wait in the evening room, please and find Morag and have tea brought in. I wish to speak with James a moment."

"Certainly." He bowed and headed to the front of the building.

She held James' hand still and walked him back across the grass to where she had been seated earlier. She then did something she never thought she would ever do. Reaching up, she placed a gentle kiss on James's lips. He did not react in shock but closed his eyes and deepened the kiss. She allowed it. Her stomach was somersaulting. Oh, how she had dreamed of kissing his lips. And at last, she was.

He stopped and placed his forehead on hers.

"Does this mean that you believe me?"

"Oh, much, much more. I have regretted every day of my life turning you down. I knew I still loved you the moment I saw you again. The empty piece of my heart suddenly filled. I still love you James." She closed her eyes and hugged him closer to her.

"I can't believe it. After all this time my dream of being with you will come true." He placed another longing kiss on her lips.

"Possibly." She sighed. "We need to become reacquainted. If after your time here you have any doubts or I have any doubts, we will call off the engagement. And I expect to be told all your plans. No secrets or spying I do not know about. Any information you get I must know. As for these men, I will accept your conclusions of their personalities. But I want to stay informed. Do you agree? These are my terms."

"If you will allow me to protect you, to stop this madness, then yes I will agree. I would also ask these men will have moments, as our relatives do now to see the love, I have for you."

She leaned up again and kissed him. "What on earth do you mean?" she added.

"I suggest you look at the evening room window." She turned and looked to see her uncle and Raeburn slapping themselves on their backs and laughing.

She laughed, and James joined in.

8

UP THE GARDEN PATH

Her hand was in his as they walked into the house and made their way to the evening room. Her uncle came and took her in his arms and lifted her from the ground.

"My darling girl. I am so excited."

"Please Uncle, let us tell you what we have decided." She giggled and straightened her dress.

"Of course, but I saw you kiss James. That alone has told me much." She drew her hand to her face feeling the heat rise to it.

James let go of her other hand and said, "Can I suggest we are all seated."

Oh, had she really kissed him? She had wanted to. But now it was unbelievable that she had. Heat climbed to her cheeks. If only she could sing out with joy and call out her beloved's name. The joy, the beating of her heart, was the same as when she had heard the announcement of Louisa's and Chalanor's engagement. This was the same joy, the excitement that surrounded her now. Her heart beating hard, the need and desire to yell out the love she had for James overtook her. This, though unexpected was what she had longed for all her life. Why no other man, even Chalanor could not capture her attention. It was only James who filled the missing piece of her heart. A piece that had disappeared when she first rejected him all those years ago. Now that piece had found its way home.

She had once thought men had wanted her only for her inheritance. The money had gone, thanks to her father and brother and the loss of the estate. James still wanted her. And it was the most important thing right now. He had always wanted her.

But what James and Lucas had told her about these other gentlemen of the Scottish elite disturbed her.

She sat next to her uncle as they explained Elspeth's terms.

"Seems reasonable, Elspeth. But might I add the two of you have been meant for each other for a long time. I knew one day you would be back together." Raeburn had never spoken so openly of his feelings, to her before. "I only wish your mothers could have seen the joy I see in your faces."

"I know my mother would have been delighted if I had accepted James ten years ago. But I was not ready. I cannot explain it. I was young and did not know my own mind." A deep sigh drifted from her.

"Our mother would have been delighted also." Added Lucas.

"Very true. She adored you, my dear, as much as I do."

"But you sound as if Lady Raeburn will not see it. James, what of your mother?"

"She died after a long illness just over a year ago."

Elspeth got up and came to sit in the seat next to James. She took his hand.

"I did not know, my dearest James."

"We had kept things quiet. Mother wanted no fuss. She passed in her sleep at our estate outside Perth. She was buried there in the family vault."

She could feel a tear run down her cheek. James lifted his hand and wiped it away.

"My dear Elspeth, you were not to know. You were going through your own grief after the loss of Freddie. But I can tell you, mother always wanted us to get back together. So, do not be sad. Her desire has come to pass."

She gave her head a shake to allow the gloom to escape. "Can I suggest, gentlemen, we gather here together this afternoon to formulate a way in which we can defend me, against these, so-called gentlemen who will arrive soon. I think I would like to be a little more prepared for this battle."

James squeezed her hand. "I think that sounds like the fighting Elspeth of old."

"Yes, it does." Added her uncle. "I had no idea these men were thinking this way. Otherwise, they would never had been invited. But now I want them to see how we protect the ones we love. And if they do not behave, I will send them on their way."

"Yes, Uncle. Now if you will excuse us, James has promised to walk with me to Portree to fetch fish for our supper."

James stood, took Elspeth by her hand.

"Let us get our coats. The clouds have rolled in and I believe the temperature has dropped."

The walk down the path to Portree was green and pleasant. The grass shone brighter as the sun hid and then revealed itself from the clouds. It was not a grand estate with manicured lawn and paths. But nature fighting with man to see who could take control. Sometimes it was man and sometimes nature. An equal battle. The day had become colder, but the sun was still shining. She and James had both brought gloves but only one hand each were dressed in the protection of leather. They held each other's hand skin against skin with the other.

They talked. She pointed out different people's houses and

spoke about who was who. She pointed out views and natural features. Which path led to where and how she loved to walk in the forest behind the town.

She shared how she had been injured at the house party and it had been an accident. She shared her love for her friends Louisa and Chalanor. How they had done what they could to protect her from the society which condemned her along with her brother. She told of her heartache at finding out the truth of what Freddie had done and at the loss of the estate.

"I am pleased that Louisa and Chalanor have remained so close to you. I must confess it was Chalanor who had been keeping an eye on you, for my benefit. He was my spy."

"You know, that does not disturb me. Chalanor was in many ways a big brother to me, even while my own brother was falling apart. I am delighted to know you have a close relationship with him."

"We do. I was doing some investigating for him up here in Scotland. You see, I found his sister. Well actually, she found me."

Elspeth stopped walking and looked at James.

"So, you chose to be the go between for Delia and Lord Farraday?"

"Yes. She has been living here in Scotland since she ran away from home some years ago. She had hidden away for some time with a relative but when word came through about her mother's death, she contacted me to help her regain contact with her brother and father. She had known we were friends and surmised correctly I would help."

They did the small amount of shopping on the wharf. So many of the locals greeted her and spoke for a moment to her. After obtaining the fish that she had wanted they headed back to the house.

People continued to greet her.

They continued to walk back up the hill to the manor house.

"How wonderful to know. Delia and I have spoken, and we plan to share more of our lives with each other. She has not returned home?"

"No but she has her reasons. I am sure she will share all with you. Now let us drop this at the kitchen and sit down with the rest of the family and sort out this battle plan."

She stopped again and leaned into James and gave him a long and lasting kiss.

"Thank you, James. This walk has been a delight and I can't wait to sit and spend more time with you."

*A*s planned, her uncle, his father and brother were all waiting for the two of them to return. He knew that their discussions would go a long way to ease her concerns. Delia had come and joined in. Lucas had filled her in with all they had discussed that morning. She seemed relieved and excited at the same time. This was good news. She knew, and believed Delia would support Elspeth as much as she could. He would talk with her later and answer any concerns that she might have.

Morag was setting out the cups for tea.

"Can you come back in half an hour, Morag, with the tea?" Elspeth was in control again and was more relaxed than he had seen her since their arrival.

Her uncle stood. "We will have Lord Farraday and his secretary as allies I believe. Sir Godfrey and his sons, Thomas and Edward, are English but very good friends of my family. So, if explained to them what might transpire, I believe we will have their support."

"Uncle that is good news. That leaves the others as possible problems."

"Elspeth, if I had known the true reason they wished to attend, I would never have agreed."

"Uncle, I mean Charles," she corrected. "This is not your problem. How on earth would you have known? But we are aware now and it means the McIntyre's and the Broderick's can be watched."

Good. Everyone was thinking on the same lines as him. What to do to protect Elspeth. She was listening carefully. He could see that. She kept glancing his way and he smiled at her encouragingly. They all needed to give her confidence and encouragement.

"That's right." he added. "We know what they are thinking so we can make it clear they will not achieve their objectives while we are here. I am determined to do all I can to protect your niece." He hoped he had conveyed to Charles the truth of his words.

"Elspeth is so much like my sister…" Charles sat down. Elspeth got up and kneeled in front of her uncle and took his hands in hers.

"We will get through this, Charles. Please do not upset yourself."

"Dear girl, you have been through so much in your young life. Many would become bitter or angry. But you have not. And it will speak volumes to anyone who takes the time to get to know you. You are the sweetest of McDonalds."

"Elspeth. If I may. I am so relieved to know you are aware of these complications. I had heard rumours and was deeply concerned for you. I was planning to tell you, but I must admit, I did not know where to begin."

Elspeth stood and came to sit next to her dear friend's sister. She lifted her hand and held it.

"I am also pleased you wanted to warn me. I do appreciate it."

He watched her as she looked at each of the people in the room. She believed their concerns and the rumours they had shared. She looked at him and he smiled at her. There was understanding between them.

"So, we watch them all very carefully. Elspeth will never be left alone. We will be her guardians. All of us. And if I may be so bold, can I suggest, Elspeth, you lock your bedroom door at night and do not open it to any of those we have concern over."

"Thank you, James. I hear and I will obey. Thank you for your care, all of you." She looked at each of them.

"Will you agree to have at least one of us near you at all times?" Lucas asked.

"Yes. I find it hard to believe these men would want to harm me. But I trust you all. So, I will do as has been suggested. Now tell me of each of the men. Their interests, their habits and such. That way I will not get drawn into a situation I cannot get out of."

He was proud of her. She listened intently as they listed various aspects of the personalities of each of the men who would soon arrive. They might not know about her, but she was determined to know everything about them.

9

THE GUESTS

The mid-August morning was cool, and the bracken was turning brown wherever the frost had laid its hand. Gazing out on the lands around her, she smiled. The rugged rocky outcrops, the large green conifers. The loch that glistened as light reflected from it surface. Skye was such a beautiful and rugged place. And she loved living here.

The rest of the guests arrive today, a thought that still troubled her. The day began early for her as she rose before the sun. She had opened her curtains to see an empty loch. That meant no one had arrived during the night. And there have not been any more ships in the loch since a few days after the night she had seen the smugglers.

Smugglers. That was such an impossibility. And what she had seen had lingered in the back of her mind since the night she had seen them. She was watching to see if anything more was happening. But so far all had been quiet.

All the gentlemen were up early too, not leaving her alone for any waking moment. They had kept their promise to always have someone near her. The previous days they had helped her prepare for all the visitors and they were able to see where they could protect her in the best way. She had spent most of her time with James and he had been wonderful and extremely useful. Both enjoyed the long walks in the forest and along isle paths. They had the opportunity to share many of the events from the ten years they had been separated. Delia was never far away. She acted as unofficial chaperone so no one would question her character. And they too had time to share their experiences. Delia had been a true friend. While the men were hunting, she planned to share more with her.

---

*A*t around nine o'clock, a ship lay anchor in the loch. Another arrived at eleven.

At noon small dinghies were ferrying the guests to shore, the place the locals called the landing. From her tower Elspeth watched. Her uncle, Charles, stood beside her.

"The first gentleman you see is Sir Godfrey. With him are his two sons. The tall gentleman on the left is Edward, his eldest. He is so different from his father. Tall and dark. I believe his mother was very tall. But he has a good nature. And the gentleman bringing in the rear is his second son, Thomas. Also, tall but like his father, blond. Though like us all, Sir Godfrey is greying now."

"Thank you, Uncle. And please let me call you uncle in private."

"Yes, my dear." He smiled at her and she gave him a hug.

"I am pleased that you can point them out to me, privately. I can then determine for myself what I am dealing with."

"My dear, do you doubt what the Raeburns have told you?"

"No uncle, just it would seem I have been a bad judge of character by all accounts, of people I thought I knew. So, I want to know my enemy, people I do not know at all and determine if they have flaws that I can see."

"Do not be so hard upon yourself, Elspeth. You were not to know of the secrets kept by your brother. Freddie had kept them from many he knew."

"That is true. But I never want to make a mistake like that again. I want to get to know these men. Not judge them as they do me but protect myself from what they might do. Especially, if I feel threatened."

"Once the Godfreys are in the house, I will take them to a private place and reveal what is going on. I have no doubt they will support us. They will not be your enemy, nor are they like others in London."

She looked at her uncle and smiled. He took her hand and gave it a little squeeze.

"The gentlemen coming up the path now are the Brodericks. Lord Broderick is from Aberdeen as is his son. But I understand the son, George, spends most of his time in Edinburgh and London. He and Oliver McIntyre are thick as thieves from what the Raeburns say."

"George is handsome. But there is something about him...I do not know. Maybe, I am imagining it. He just makes me feel uncomfortable. But who is the other young man?"

"I do not know. He has no brother. Perhaps...no, he is in gentleman attire. We will find out. Do not fret. I will get James to be with you when they arrive."

She heard a carriage pull up in the drive below. She looked down. "This must be the McIntyres."

"Yes. They must have come in at the fishing village, Portree. Strange. But it does not matter. Now prepare yourself, my dear. And do not fret. We will prevail."

*J*ames was waiting for her as she came down the stairs. The servants were in the foyer greeting the new arrival and directing the servants of the visitors to the various rooms in the house. Her uncle went and accompanied the Godfreys to their rooms. She and James came into the foyer just as the McIntyres came in.

"James, my dear fellow…" Oliver came to shake his hand.

"Arrived already?" His smile seemed genuine.

"Have been here a number of days actually. May I introduce to you Miss Elspeth Ismay, my fiancé."

And there it was. As clear to her as rain. A snarl and a frown upon his face. It was there but a moment, long enough for her to see it if she was looking. Which she certainly was.

She gave the man a curtsy. He returned a bow. "Well, well, I had no idea you two even knew each other."

"We have known each other all our lives." She responded before James could reply. James picked up her hand and kissed her fingers. He gave a smile of approval to her, which she returned.

She looked steadily at Oliver. He was tall like James but not as handsome. He was also somewhat reckless in his appearance. He was unshaven and his hair could do with a good comb.

"Oh, Father, come and meet Miss Ismay. James is engaged to this lovely lady." She may have imagined it, but it seemed that comment was almost sarcastic. James must have thought so too, as he gave her hand a little squeeze.

"Miss Ismay." Sir Chester bowed and looked at her with disdain. "I believe you are the chatelaine here."

"Yes, Sir McIntyre. I am also the niece of Charles MacDonald, your host."

He gave his head a little shake and the gloom that seemed to be in his eyes was gone.

"Just so, just so. My dear."

Oliver's father was not as tall but straight and well presented. Not a hair was out of place. A man of distinction at least in his presentation.

"Morag, will you please take Sir McIntyre and Mr Oliver to their rooms, please?"

"Yes ma'am." She smiled at Morag who had placed great emphasis on the 'ma'am'. She then let go of James' hand and walked past them to greet the other arrivals. James followed and came to walk beside her.

"James, old boy. How wonderful to see you!" George Broderick trumpeted.

"George." He bowed "May I introduce you to Miss Elspeth Ismay."

She curtsied. She smiled and received a huge smile in return.

"I had no idea that we would have a lovely lady here. What do you think, Alexander? Oh, I am sorry may I introduce you to Alexander Thompson."

The tall and dark-haired man bowed and then looked directly at her. This was the unexpected guest. She questioned herself for a moment. Those deep brown eyes? Had she seen them before?

"Miss Ismay, I believe I knew your brother Fredrick?"

"You may have, sir."

"We also met. You were much younger."

"I am sorry, sir, but I have no recollection." Which was true for she could not remember or place him. The eyes were familiar but how and where had she met him?

"I don't believe we have met either." James placed his hand out towards this dark stranger. "I am James Raeburn, Elspeth's fiancé."

The stranger's smile lifted on one side, ever so briefly.

"Our loss, George." He added.

A shiver ran up and down her back. It was not cold. Her body was shaking but not from any cold. Him standing there disturbed her equilibrium. It was called fear. She grabbed at James' hand. He squeezed it back. Maybe he sensed her tension?

"Luncheon will be served in an hour. Morag?" who had just come back down the stairs. "Please take these gentlemen to their rooms, if you please."

"Yes ma'am."

The gentlemen followed the maid towards the stairs.

"James," she paused and looked at her beloved. "We will wait in the evening room."

"Yes, my dear."

As they walked towards the evening room, she heard the dark stranger say to George. "You can see who the master of the relationship will be. Or should I say mistress." And he chuckled.

In the evening room, he took Elspeth into his arms. "Do not listen to them."

"I have no intention of doing so." She hugged him back.

"Do you remember Alexander?"

"No. But there is something niggling in the back of my mind. I just can't put my finger on it."

"It will come to you. Just do not think on it too much. Let me know if you remember. I will ask Lucas if he knows of him and will let you know."

He escorted her to a seat and sat next to her.

"It's his eyes I remember. But I cannot think of what context I remember them." She shivered. "Never mind. But I do not like him. That much I know. He gives me a terrible feeling in the pit of my stomach. And a chill up my spine. And it is not pleasant. I actually fear him."

"Another good reason to stay away from him." He took her hand

and lifted it to his fingers. She watched as he placed a kiss on her fingertips and smiled.

"Now if eyes are what you want to talk about, then have I ever told you, your eyes are the colour of bluebells?"

She looked at him and grinned. "I do believe you told me that when we first met, as children."

———

The gentlemen had all come into the evening room and sat where they could. Others stood by the windows gazing at the scenery surrounding them. She said nothing but could hear various comments of *desolate, wilderness, forgotten, lack of society and desperate*. To them it might feel so, but she loved the isle and was controlling her temper as it grew in disgust of their comments. What if they were talking of her? Her stomach dropped again.

She watched them as they glanced in her and James' direction as the comments were made. What they did not know was—she was watching them intently as well. Determining their natures, stature, and behaviours. Many had gone very quickly down in her estimation. They were not pleasant. They lacked civility.

She hesitated for a moment, whispered in James' ear, and then stood. She excused herself and left the room.

———

He understood why she left. So many men and their attentions were directed at her. She needed to leave before she was overwhelmed. Knowing her as he did, she would gladly give them a piece of her mind. And she did not want to embarrass her uncle.

Some of them may reveal a little more if she was not here. He would rather have her by his side, but all these males were enough to drive her to her room for the remainder of the day. She would be safe as she had promised to lock the door. He would go and check on her later. Sir Godfrey and his two sons Edward and Thomas came to stand around him. Sir Godfrey sat where Elspeth had just been.

"May I congratulate you on your engagement to Miss Elspeth?"

He heard a grunt coming from the direction of the window but could not make out who had made the disparaging noise.

"Thank you, Sir Godfrey. I appreciate it greatly."

"She is a strong and thoughtful woman and most beautiful."

The grunt was heard again, and he was sure it came from George who was standing at the window with Oliver.

"She is most beautiful, and I have always thought so." He replied, returning his gaze to the gentlemen around him. "She has always been well accepted in company until her brother's fall from grace."

"Such a tragedy, people condemning her for her brother's actions." Edward added.

Oliver and George made their way towards him.

"Surely, you cannot believe she did not know what her brother was up to?" George intervened. "She lived in the same house as him since their parents had died. Begs the question as to whether the accident which occurred to her parents was truly an accident."

Clenching his jaw, James stared at him. He wanted to hit him and hit him hard. George did not know anything about Elspeth or her family. How dare he speak like this? Even though his mouth was dry, he took a deep breath to control himself before he spoke.

"I find it strange that you would comment on a person you had never met until today. And on the relationships, she has had with her family, a family you have never met."

Alexander came over to join in the discussion.

"It would be true of these gentlemen but not of me, James. I knew Freddie very well."

"Then I am surprised you did not warn society of his behaviour before he murdered those women." He watched Alexander smirk at him. "If he hid his behaviour from you, perhaps then he hid it from his sister. A sister who adored him until his demise. She need not be punished by you, sirs; she daily asks why she did not see any sign."

He walked over to him and stood before him. He was breathing hard. His fingers twitched as his fists opened and closed. He lifted his fist and wanted to hit him in the face. No. He would not do it. He held himself back. Only a thread stood between him and the moment he would snap. But he would not get away with these comments. So, he used his words instead.

"If you knew him then you are as much to blame for his actions as you are prepared to attach to his sister. I suggest you look at yourself before you condemn Miss Elspeth."

"Well said." added Sir Godfrey.

At that moment, Morag entered and announced the arrival of Lord Faraday and his secretary. Sir Godfrey and his sons, as well as he, moved away from Alexander to greet the new arrivals. Alexander came uninvited yet he dared to question Elspeth? Could he not see that she was protected and supported? They all had made it very clear.

The vixen has retreated. Scared or does she feel guilty? Alexander went back to the window to look at the wilderness.

I wonder if she had put together her thoughts and remembered the last time, she had seen him?

Probably not. But she would eventually. Then she would be filled with fear. And he loved the fear.

He had desired to have her body many times over the years.

With Freddie around he did not dare to try. But now? He would not let James be her first. Watching her days ago from the ship had reinforced his desire for her. Waiting in Portree for George to pick him up before they sailed into the loch had driven him almost mad. He had even seen her walking into the village with her ridiculous James.

Freddie had been reckless. He would not be so. Their type of interest had made them a group of special men. Freddie was the first to be found out and had died a terrible death. But he knew that others were ready to do the same as he and Freddie. They would just be more discreet about it. It was their right after all. Women were there for man's pleasure and nothing more.

10

———

DELIA

$\mathcal{D}$elia joined Elspeth in her room. Even she was reluctant to enter the room with all those men. The ladies were happy in each other's company.

Elspeth allowed the gentlemen to have luncheon on their own. Delia and she had a small luncheon in her room. It would allow the men to plan and discuss the hunting over the coming days. She could not shake the fact that she might be on the list of game.

Finally, she asked Delia her thoughts and what she had heard of the rumours.

"Yes, I have heard them. This is why I would rather be here with you; those men scare me. When any of my real friends brought it up, I corrected their thoughts. Having known you all my life I knew you could not have turned into the monster they were trying to create. But with some people I did not have the courage to speak up. They believed themselves to be an authority."

"On me?"

"Yes, on you. Except when I asked, they did not know you."

"Well, that convinces me if nothing else did. You are a sweet girl. And I thank you for defending me when you could."

"Then James told me you were coming here. My father revealed he too was going to attend before coming to see me. So, I asked James if he and his family would mind if I came along."

"I imagine he said yes straight away."

"He did. And I sent a missive to my father to tell him. He also was delighted. James let your uncle know but I am not sure the message arrived before we did."

"As far as I know, it did not. But I am delighted by the surprise."

"I am, too. It is a pleasure to see you again."

Elspeth stood and poured Delia some more tea.

"I would like to hear what you have been doing since you left Kent. And how you have stayed hidden for so long." She returned to her seat.

"Well, let me begin from when I left home. Mother had told me my father was not my father. I begged her to tell me who my real father was. She would not. All she hinted at was she had fallen pregnant with me when they had visited relatives in Scotland. I pestered her for days, but she ignored me. She would not acknowledge me or say a word to me."

"That is terrible. You poor dear."

"I went to my room and did not come out. Father wanted to talk to me, but I refused. I was so angry at my mother. I got my stubbornness from her at least, but I doubted everything about myself. I wrote to a distant aunt, who I had held in high regard. I asked if I could come and I had a one-word reply. 'Come.' The one word was all she wrote. So, with the help of some of the servants, who understood my heart, I fled by carriage to the boarder. From there I arranged a carriage to my aunt's. I did not want the servants to be compromised. This way they could honestly say they did not know where I was. My maid servant came with me. She did not want to stay at Maidstone."

"You seemed to think of everything."

"My heart was broken, and my aunt was the tonic I needed to

help me mend. She did not appreciate what her half-sister had done. I stayed with her and talked through all with her. But she could not enlighten me to who my real father was. She did not know for certain. She had clues but nothing definite. So, we determined we had a few avenues of finding out who it might be. I needed to know. Well, it is what I thought at the time."

"I had no idea your mother had a half-sister. She never spoke of her."

"Mother said she was the black sheep of the family. It is not the impression I witnessed."

"I understand your need to know who your real father is. Have you been able to find out?"

"No, but we have hired a man who is investigating the time and place where I know my mother and father and Chalanor had visited. My aunt has been happy to sponsor me. In fact, she has made me her heir. It is no great fortune, but I can survive without any help. If he can find out who my real father is, then I will go to him if I can. But things have changed."

"Your mother being killed, by my brother. Do you hate me?"

"Elspeth, I am a grown woman. I am almost twenty years of age. I understand what my mother was like and just how many men she had taken to her bed. She brought her death on herself. She did not take care. They may be harsh words, but they are true. I do not blame you for your brother's deed. I do not even blame him completely. My mother could be a difficult woman."

"Your mother did not deserve to die in the manner she did."

"I agree, but I need to blot out that part of the story. I am yet to come to terms with her demise. She has gone without telling me who my father is. And with her gone it allows me to find out more. I wrote to father and explained my reasons for not returning and he understood. A gentler and understanding man I know not of. He hoped I would come home but I am not yet ready. I still acknowledge him as my father, and he raised me. But I need to find my true lineage. I have given myself a few more years to search."

"Lord Farraday had a difficult time himself. His wound was grievous. We believe my brother's manservant was the one who shot the arrow. But he disappeared not long after the event. He has not been seen since."

Elspeth stood and walked to the window and looked out over the loch.

"Your father is the kindest of men."

"My dear papa is kind and understanding. He sent all of Mother's diaries to me, so I could go through them. I wanted to see if she mentioned something of who my father was. We have been going through them. But the ones from the time she would have fallen pregnant are not there. I believe after I left my mother may have destroyed them. So, I would never know."

"But then why have you not returned to Kent?" She came and sat again.

"That is a little more complicated. You see, I have met a gentleman with whom I have deep feelings. Unfortunately, he sees me as a girl and not a woman. I want to see if I can win his heart."

"Oh, and do we know him?"

"His family are friends with ours. But they have helped to keep my secret. And I am truly grateful. If you do not mind, I will keep his identity a secret. I have told no one. I do not want rumour to get back to him."

"Of course. I hope that your interest will be recognised."

"But enough of me. Please tell me what you have been doing since the tragedy of your brother…"

"Ahh… Sadness reigned. I could not believe my brother had done such a terrible thing. But he was dead. I was now alone. Well, that is not quite true. Your brother and father did much to help me as did my uncle. But it is strange to think I am the last of my immediate family. There are no others."

"And what of love? Did you not think of my brother at one time?"

"No and yes. My love for him was of a sister to her brother. We were close but there was no spark, you could say, between us. We were both romantics and believed we would know when we found love. We just did not see each other in the romantic sense. Your brother had deep feelings for Louisa, and I encouraged him in those feelings. As for me, no one has filled the part of my heart James once did."

"So, this pretend engagement might actually lead to a real one?"

"In some respects, I hope so. But we have not seen each other for a long time. We need to become reacquainted with each other. So far he is still James but now more mature."

"Thank you for allowing me to be part of this situation. I promise I will do what I can to help you."

"Thank you, Delia. I appreciate it. Perhaps this rumour will prove all talk and no substance."

*L*ater in the afternoon James brought Lord Farraday to see them in private. As Lord Farraday entered the room Delia stood and then threw herself into her father's arms.

"Papa, Papa." She said, repeatedly. They held each other. Elspeth wanted to give them time alone so quietly stepped out of her room onto the landing. James was waiting there for her.

11

———

REUNITED

"You look tired." He took her into his embrace.

"Yes. We have shared a lot this afternoon. But it was enlightening for us both. Delia has grown into a special young lady. Her father and brother will be proud. She is not like her mother in any way. Her personality is her own. Her appearance must be of her real father. Lord and Lady Farraday both have dark hair. Thou his lordship is turning grey."

"She is a true member of the ton despite her parentage. Lord Farraday, I am sure will always see her as his own." He leaned down and placed a gentle kiss on her cheek. Then on her lips. Then the kiss deepened.

"Uh hum. Sorry to intrude. But really? I never thought I would find you lurking in the corridors."

James turned around. It was George. He wanted to protect Elspeth, so he moved in front of her.

"What are you doing here?" He sounded rough and menacing even to his own ears.

"Just having a look around, old boy. No need for the hackles."

"These stairs only come to my room, Mr Broderick." Elspeth

stepped around him and placed her hands on her hips. "But I believe your intention was to find out, wasn't it? There is no need or excuse for you to be here. Please leave."

"I do apologise ma'am." He smirked. "As I said I was but looking around. I will depart."

"And don't let me see you here again." She added.

After a moment when he was sure that George had gone, he again took her into his arms.

"Well said, my dear. I think that he might have understood that message."

"I can only hope." And she kissed him. A kiss he deepened and enjoyed.

———

It was funny to be sitting on the step outside her room. She wanted to be nearby in case either Lord Farraday or Delia needed her. After a short time, Lord Farraday came to the door and bid them to come in.

They entered and found Delia with a broad smile and with colour in her cheeks. She stood and gave her father a peck on his cheek.

"I will go and have a rest before we prepare for dinner."

She came over to Elspeth. "Thank you for sharing all with me and allowing me to speak with you. I am truly grateful."

"As am I." They gave each other a gentle hug and Delia left the room.

"My dearest girl. I am appalled at what you are facing here. James has made me aware of what is taking place. You will have my unswerving support. You cannot and will not be blamed for your brother's actions. Not in my presence."

"Dear, Lord Farraday, I appreciate your concern. But I am

hoping that this has been over emphasised, and it will disappear with the morning breeze."

"Very poetic my dear, but I will stand by you, regardless of what anyone or anything might be said or done to diminish you." He stood proud and strong. He had become such a strong and supportive man since the terrible events of a year ago.

"Thank you, my lord, but please tell me how my dear friends Chalanor and Louisa are doing?"

He relaxed a little and she indicated to him to sit on the chaise at the other side of the bedroom. She followed and sat next to him. James sat at the end of her bed. Doing such distracted her for a moment, but she returned her attention to his lordship.

"Very well, my dear. I have been asked to inform you that Louisa is with child. Expecting the arrival in the new year. I wished to tell you in person. But here is a letter from them telling you of their joy and excitement." He handed her the missive from inside his coat pocket.

Elspeth gave the lord a hug which he returned with gusto.

He continued. "I am so pleased joy has returned to the estate. Everyone is excited. Also, we have found Delia. I hope she will return with me for a visit at least."

"I am so glad I could be here to witness your reunion. She seems very happy."

"She is, my dear. I am off to Edinburgh after the hunt to meet with her aunt. I know she wishes to stay in Scotland for a while. She will always remain my daughter despite what her mother has declared."

"Yes, she always will."

"But I had to see you and give you the good news. We will expect you to return to us to visit once the baby has arrived."

"I am sure I will, my lord."

"But for now, know I will watch over you as if you were my

own daughter. And I dare any man to say a discouraging word of you in my presence. They will deal with my anger and fury."

She took his hand and knew he would be her biggest defender. She had known him for most of her life and he was such a wonderful man.

"I received word by letter two days ago and was asked to keep it a surprise, so Lord Farraday could make the announcement. To see you both together at this moment makes me very happy I waited." James said.

"So, you knew? I am glad. And I must say that it is most welcomed. My joy for Chalanor and Louisa is complete. After all they have been through, I rejoice in this wonderful news." She smiled at the two gentlemen. She was happy for them but deep in her heart she asked again if such joy would ever befall her.

James escorted her to her seat.

"But I need to ask if you are in good spirits? You left suddenly this morning."

"I am. But being surrounded by all the gentlemen, did make me feel a little overwhelmed. Listening to them, disturbed me. But I have determined I will stay away from them as much as I can. I will breakfast on my own. And will only sit with you all at dinner and after. This will allow all to relax and will not place so much pressure on me. Besides, most of your time will be involved in the hunting. Which should keep me out of the trouble we have envisaged."

Lord Farraday stood up and, "May I make a suggestion?"

"Of course, your lordship." She looked up into his now stern face.

"I would suggest, my dear, you are everywhere we are in the house. If you stay away, then the men who are against you will think they can control you. Believe me my dear, I speak from experience. And you have Delia here now and her presence may keep them quiet. You are not alone despite what they might think."

She lowered her gaze to her lap.

"James has said the same thing. I agree, reluctantly. My heart says no but my head agrees with you. I cannot let them think they affect me. This last day I can rule out as being busy getting all things in place. Very well, gentlemen. I agree."

She stood and took both men into her embrace.

Her strength of character never failed to impress James. She doubted herself. And it concerned him. She had never doubted herself before. The toll Freddie had taken on her was terrible and obvious to him. But her strength seemed as if it was returning. She could master this situation as she had many others over the years.

He and Lord Farraday left her so that she could dress for dinner.

James came for her an hour later and escorted her down to dinner. Refreshed and determined to not allow these so-called men to treat her badly, she walked on air beside James. She knew she had the support of several of the guests. As they came through the dining room door, the men stood. Alexander and George were to be sitting opposite from her. She was glad of this as she could then try to piece together where and when she had met Alexander. And if he really did know her brother as he said he did.

12

PLEASE LOVE ME

The meal was again a resounding success. Some of the gentlemen wished to thank her for the effort but she soon made it clear the cook Mrs Mc Dougal was the creator of the feast.

They retired to the evening room. Whisky was available as was tea. Some of the men chose to play cards. She sat with her tea and with James, her uncle, Delia, and Lord Farraday.

"May I introduce you to Mr Arthur Thomas, Miss Elspeth?"

She bowed her head at the dark-haired man in front of her.

He bowed to her.

"It is my pleasure to meet you, Miss Elspeth. Lord Farraday speaks very highly of you."

A grunt came from the men playing cards.

"I will not stand for this." Her uncle had stood and in no uncertain terms had shown his displeasure. "If I hear any more grunts, groans or any other comments against my niece, you gentlemen can depart this lodge post haste. Do I make myself clear?"

No one responded. And she was sure no one would. They

wanted her on her own, so they could disgrace her privately. They knew now that her uncle would not stand for any misbehaviour. There would be no more grunts or groans. Very little was in fact said for the remainder of the evening. The men soon excused themselves using the early start the following morning as a chance to get away from the stillness which had descended on the company.

Delia promised to see her at breakfast later in the morning and then excused herself and went to bed.

"It would appear we are finally alone, my dear." James chuckled. "Are you sure you wish for me to go on the hunt? I can stay here with you?"

"No, James. It would be best you did some hunting. I need to do some preparations for the coming week and Delia has promised not to leave my side. Besides, I think all the men are going on the hunt. I am sure I will be quite safe."

"Very well then, can I escort you to the stairs of your tower?"

"No need, my dear. I want to check on the staff and make sure all is ready for your early breakfast."

"Then, my love," he lifted her hand, "All that is left is for me to wish you a good night's sleep." He kissed her fingers, bowed, and took his leave.

He was only gone a few moments when Alexander came back into the room.

"I say, all alone?"

"No sir, I have rung the bell and am awaiting the arrival of the maid."

Morag entered the room.

"Yes ma'am?"

"Morag, can you pack away the tea and whisky dishes please. And check with the cook and be sure all is in readiness for the early breakfast. And let me know in my room if there is anything to report. I am retiring to my room."

"Yes ma'am." She curtsied and began to collect the dishes around the room and place them on the table in the corner.

"Goodnight, Mr. Thompson." She went past him. He took her arm as she went by and not very gently.

"Call me Alexander. You always did."

"Please let go of my arm, sir. I still have no recollection of our acquaintance."

He let go of her arm, while looking deeply into her eyes.

"Let me remind you, the waterfall."

She stared at him, shook her head, and left. Waterfall, waterfall. It made no sense at all.

The sun was shining, and the only thing she could hear was the waterfall. As she got closer, she became more excited. Was she going to see them swimming? She wanted to go with them, but they would not let her. They said she was too young to be with them. After all they were grown men. She frowned. They were not men. Freddie was only fifteen. She was twelve and more grown up than they thought.

She could hear them splashing in the pool under the falls. She found a place where they would not see her. They were swimming around. She watched for a moment. They seemed happy. But she could not understand why she could not have joined in.

Her brother stood up on the rock near the falling water. He was naked. She covered her mouth with her hand, shocked. She had never seen him with no clothes on before. When he swam with her, he always left on his trousers.

Then Alexander stood next to him. He too was naked. She could not take her eyes from him. His body shone with the water reflecting off him. She noticed he started to fondle his penis. It was growing. She drew in a long breath and held it. She hoped they had not heard her. Now he touched Freddie and Freddie in return fondled him.

From behind the waterfall came a woman. She was older. Her long black wet hair clung to her naked body. She was beautiful. She had full plump breasts. Was this how she would look one day? And would the men want her the way Alexander and Freddie wanted the lady? They could not stop looking at her. Lusting after her? She came to the boys and with her hands started to caress their bodies. They in turn suckled on her breasts and sucked on all other parts of her body.

Her eyes were glued to their movements and actions. She could not take her eyes off them. This must be what sex is. Playing with others' body parts. She listened to the lady groan and the boys were moaning too. They were enjoying the actions.

They took the black-haired beauty to the edge of the pond. They helped her lay down. Then Alexander pushed his erect penis into the woman. She moaned again and seemed to like what he had done. She moaned louder and louder. Moans of deep pleasure. She screamed...

Elspeth sat upright in her bed. She was sweating. My God, she remembered. Alexander was a friend of Freddie's when he was around fifteen.

As a mere twelve year old herself, she had wanted Alexander to do to her what he had done to the black-haired beauty. Now as an adult, remembering that strange moment in her life, she shook her head. A hot flush of heat went through her. She was ashamed. She had been aroused by Alexander's actions. And his beautiful body. Even now her vagina was thumping as the blood rushed to it. She yearned for release.

Her eyes saw James in her mind, and the heat was still rushing and thumping through her. My God, she wanted James. She wanted him to make her scream. She was aroused beyond anything she had experienced before.

She got up and opened the curtain allowing the moon light to light her room enough for her to find her dressing gown and put it on.

Alexander had said waterfall before she had gone to bed, and it would seem, it was enough for her to remember the event. But how had he known she was there? Had he known all these years? She had never told even her brother. But somehow Alexander knew she had been there.

She had to admit that as a young girl, she had been attracted to him. But she could not remember the last time she had seen him. It was obvious from the actions of her brother and Alexander that day, they had maintained a close friendship, which involved sex and more sex.

When Alexander said he knew her brother well, she did not doubt it. Not for a moment since she remembered the waterfall. But had he gone down the same twisted path her brother had? Was he also having sex with a woman and then just killing her? Having the feelings of wanting James near her was only natural. The thought of Alexander doing to her what he had done to the black-haired beauty made her shudder. His actions were not love. It was just sex. If Alexander tried to do it with her…she shuddered again.

Wanting James to revive her and remove the tension in her body, she could not go back to sleep. Her mind was racing, and she needed to talk with him. Her love for him was growing. She felt drawn to him and repulsed by her attraction as a twelve-year-old to Alexander. She wanted to see James and tell him of her dream.

She left her room, determined to tell him what she had experienced. She could not wait. She tiptoed to his room and gently tapped on his door. For a few breathless moments she waited for him to answer. He did. He pulled her into the room.

"Elspeth my dear, what is the matter? Why are you here? Are you all right?"

"I needed to speak with you, but not here. Please come back with me to my room. I must speak with you. I remember."

Moments later they were making their way up the stairs to her room.

She closed the door and locked it as had been her practice since the guests had arrived.

He took her into his arms. "My darling Elspeth, what is it? You seem distressed?"

"I am. I finally remembered where and when Alexander and my brother were acquainted. Wait a moment and I will tell all."

She took a deep breath as she clung to him. She told him of the encounter with Alexander and of her dream. She drew strength from him being with her and listening to what she had to say. She did not hide her feelings or the concern she had. Alexander knew she had seen them. What a shock.

"Did your brother ever talk about the day with you?"

"No. It is the strangest thing. I am sure he never knew I was there. He would have scolded me if he had known."

"Well, can you remember other details? What happened in real life, I mean after you woke up?"

She closed her eyes and rested her forehead on James' chest.

"You know I cannot remember."

"Are you sure it really happened? Perhaps it is just a bad dream."

"I thought it could be, but now I know, I remembered what took place. I think I blocked it out because I was so ashamed of seeing what I saw and feeling what I felt. I was but a child."

"Very well. Then perhaps more details will come to you as you remember the event. Do not fret. We now know how he was acquainted with your brother. I will attempt to find out how long that acquaintance existed. After all he may have had nothing more to do with him. I have been in discussion with Chalanor and we are looking at the past of your brother and all his acquaintances. He may come up with more information."

"I know that Freddie went to Oxford not long after the waterfall experience and that Alexander went also. But after that, I am ignorant of their relationship."

He hugged her closer. His arms around her provided security and she started to breathe easier.

"You understand, don't you?"

"I think so. This has awoken part of you, a part you have kept buried away."

"Yes and no. Yes, to the event but it has awoken something else in me. My desire to make love with you. To cement the love, we have always had. To be truly yours."

He lifted her chin and kissed her mouth. The blood rushed to the area of her body where she had wanted to feel him inside her. She moaned into his mouth. She eased away from the kiss.

He looked into her eyes. "You must know I want you more than you can imagine. But we are not yet married."

"I don't care. I want to feel you inside me, now. I am a woman of control, as you know. If I want you, you can be sure it is the greatest desire of my heart."

"I do not doubt you, my love. So, I will make love to you with my hands and mouth but not yet with what I desire most to do to you. I will see your uncle tomorrow and we will arrange for a special licence. We can marry immediately. But I must protect your reputation from these men. Please my darling, agree."

She knew he was right. If these men found out she and James were making love, her reputation would be even lower than it was. As he had come to her to protect her, she agreed. Though deep in her heart she wanted him naked in her bed. And one day soon it will happen.

"But for now, let me give you a taste of my plans for your body."

He swooped her into his arms, and she gave a little squeal of delight. Her heart was beating faster with every passing second. He carried her to her bed and laid her on it. He sat next to her and reached down and undid the buttons at the front of her night shirt. He cupped her breasts with his hands. Then with his mouth, caressed her nipples. She moaned and the blood pulsated hard between her legs. His administrations were heaven. Why had she ever rejected him? They could be making love right now if she had only said yes years ago.

His hand went under her shirt and found the cleft between her legs. He gently opened the gap. She could feel the hot moisture there. His hand found her point of pleasure and she exploded. His mouth caught the scream of delight from her mouth. His fingers reached into the moisture and began to rub and move back and forth. She went with him, reaching higher and higher with the pleasure he gave.

She screamed her release into his mouth as his tongue gently stroked her tongue and lips. He lifted her into his embrace and kissed her till she slumped sated in his arms.

"Sleep, my love, and dream only of me and what I will do to you for the rest of our lives. I love you."

What a revelation. She needed and wanted him, and he had just proved what he can make her experience. He was filled with love for her and she loved him back at last. Waiting all these years until she was ready only increased his sensations. The pleasure he had bestowed on her. He wanted to give her, each day for as long as they lived. Sex be dammed. To give her pleasure was the greatest thing. To see and feel her on the heights of pleasure at his hands. He wanted all of it for her.

He covered her with the blanket from her bed. Kissing her warmed honeyed lips one more time, he slowly tiptoed from the room. He walked back to his room.

Soon they would wed.

lexander watched him come from the tower stairs. Damn the man. He must already have had her. This was not what he wanted. He wanted to ravage her as he had dreamed of doing since he saw her at the waterfall. The lust she had in her eyes at the waterfall had kept him wanting her. The memory of her aroused him. He closed the door and went back to bed. Morag was but a substitute, and a poor one at best. But he drew her into his arms and placed his member inside her. He pictured Elspeth and rammed his release into the servant. It would have to do for now.

13

A WONDERFUL DAY

Her curtains were open. She usually had them closed. Rolling over, she stretched. Then she remembered his hand in her private place and the pleasure he had bestowed upon her. She should be ashamed for allowing him the privilege. But she was not. She had never felt so loved, so cared for. He had forgone his own pleasure to pour out delights upon her. It was wonderful.

She got out of bed and walked over to the window. The sun was dawning to the east. She could see the gentlemen below getting into the wagon to take them on the hunting trip into the hills. James looked to her window and blew her a kiss. They would marry and soon, and she was delighted at the thought.

She looked at the other gentleman and her eye rested on Alexander. His piercing gaze was on her. She tried to look away but could not. For in his look was pure evil. Nothing had ever been more certain to her. The man was evil and meant to do her harm. She would tell her James when they got back. Her James. The sound gave her pleasure. To know they would soon be together was a delight.

Moving to her desk she picked up her journal. She sat down.

But instead of writing in pencil she chose to write in ink. She explained her dream. What it might mean. Her desperate desire to see James last night. The pleasure he poured out on her. Wanting to marry and the pure evil she had seen this morning, in the eyes of a man she was only beginning to remember. But not something she wanted to know about.

"Good morning, Elspeth." It was nice to be greeted by a friendly face.

"Good morning, Delia. I hope you slept well."

"I did. I am most refreshed."

"Good morning, Miss Elspeth and Miss Delia." It was Mr Thomas, Lord Farraday's secretary.

"Good morning, Mr Thomas. Did you not want to go hunting?"

"No madam, I did not. I am afraid the pastime does nothing for me. I am here to help Lord Farraday. I have a few letters to write on his behalf today. And I will take a walk into town later and see what Portree is made of. And ladies call me Arthur if you please."

"Very well Arthur. I can point out a few other attractions that you could visit if Lord Farraday is occupied. Do you ride?"

"I do."

"Then we will arrange a horse for you if you desire."

"Thank you, ma'am. I will be sure to ask if the need arises."

"Sir, may I ask you a question?" Delia seemed nervous. She was wringing her hands as she asked.

"Certainly, Miss Delia. What can I do to help?"

"How is my father really? I mean since the accident."

Arthur looked pensive. But he replied. "Well miss, I was hired after the accident as his lordship was in a bad way and could do nothing with his arm. It took many months for him to heal and slowly regain the use of it. However, it became clear my service might be needed for a longer period of time. It pains him greatly to put pen or pencil to paper. Unfortunately, his arm will never be quite the same again."

"So, when you write, are you using his words or yours?"

Elspeth suddenly realised what Delia meant. What she was concerned about.

"Oh, miss do not fret. The business letters I write, and he adds his signature. I listen to him and write the words he says and then he signs your letters. Whatever he says, miss, is from him. And I will keep them private."

"That is good to know. Thank you, Mr Thomas." Her sigh of relief was audible to them both.

"Please miss, call me Arthur."

"Thank you, Arthur."

She watched Arthur smile at Delia. He had eased her mind. She could also see Arthur had concerns for Delia. He wanted to put her at ease. She had noticed the blushing smile from Delia and could see she was more relaxed. They enjoyed a pleasurable breakfast together.

Her jobs for the day were minimal. Lunch had been packed in picnic baskets to be taken to the men in the hills later in the morning. All was prepared.

Her dear uncle had hired two more maids who had reduced much of the extra work she had to do. He had also hired some of the isles men to go with the gentlemen on the hunt. They would skin and prepare any of the deer shot. Including preparing and mounting any heads the men wanted to keep. She liked to see deer heads on walls but would prefer to see them on the live animals, walking the forest. Hunting disturbed her. If it was for food, she understood it. But to obtain a head as a trophy, she could not see why they had to destroy such a beautiful animal.

*L*uncheon was just the three of them again. But as the lunch was brought out, her uncle came and sat down. A maid added an extra table setting.

"Charles, is everything alright?"

"Perfect, my dear. I was on an errand for James. A very wonderful errand."

She could feel the heat rising to her cheeks. She knew he had gone for the special licence.

"Now let us sit and enjoy this beautiful meal."

"Who then is hosting the hunt if you are here?" she asked.

"James is leading them for me. I knew that obtaining the licence would be easier for me to get as I am known here on the isle."

"Licence. A special licence?" asked Delia, looking at her expectantly.

"Yes. I do not wish to wait. I waited years and do not wish to wait any longer."

"Oh, how wonderful." Arthur was smiling from ear to ear. "May I be the first to congratulate you, Miss Elspeth. How wonderful. I am very excited for you."

"As am I, my dear Elspeth. This is truly delightful news."

"Thank you both. Can I ask you to keep it to yourselves for the time being until James and I can work out what we will do next? Then we can announce it."

"Rest assured your secret is safe with us," continued Arthur. "This is truly a joyous occasion."

"That it is," added her uncle. "A day I have waited for."

"As have I. Thank you, uncle." A wide smile spread across her face. She had not smiled in over a year.

They continued the meal in general discussion. Then the sounds of a great commotion out at the front of the building came through the open doors.

Morag came running into the dining room.

"Miss, sir. You must come quickly. One man is hurt."

"What has happened?" her uncle asked as he stood and placed his napkin on the table.

"One of the men has been shot. Tis all I know. They are bringing him in the wagon to the front door as we speak." She was almost in tears.

"Who is it, Morag?"

"I dunna know, mistress." She turned and fled the room.

She stood from the table and headed quickly out to the front door just as the wagon was pulling up. Lucas and James were seated in the back of the wagon.

"Who is hurt, my love," Elspeth called as she dashed to the wagon.

"I am, my dear. But it is not bad."

"What on earth happened?" She grabbed his hand as he reached out to her.

The other gentlemen were walking up the wide driveway the wagon had just come up.

"It is supposed to be an accident, but I do not believe it for a moment." Added Lucas. He helped his brother move towards the back of the cart. Lucas stood and jumped off the cart and then helped his brother down.

Elspeth came to him and held him close. "Where, my dear?"

"My leg. A bullet grazed it and hit a rock behind me. The rock exploded and I have minor scratches from the rock bits that flew out. Several of them also penetrated my leg, but I am alright."

"But you are covered in blood. How on earth could it be minor wounds?"

"That is because of me, Elspeth." Lucas took her hand. "I was carrying a deer I had shot and dropped it next to James when I came rushing to him. The blood from the deer seeped into his clothes."

Her uncle had his hands on his hips. "Who shot you?" His voice was low and menacing.

"Alexander." Lucas answered.

They all looked at each other. She could feel the heat rising on her face. But she was also scared. Had Alexander done this deliberately?

"That was no accident." She fumed. "I saw evil in his eyes this morning. Now I know why."

Alexander and the other men had reached the cart.

"Hysterical woman. Evil. My God, you are a crazy woman. Your brother taught you well." Alexander had his gun flopped over his shoulder. The other men from Edinburgh who she knew to be part of the plot against her, gathered around Alexander in some show of defiance. She went over and slapped him across the face. He laughed at her.

"I have had enough of this." Her uncle stated clearly. "You have been trouble from the beginning." He pointed at Alexander. "And you, sir, were not even invited. I allowed you to stay out of respect for the Brodericks. I now ask the Brodericks and McIntyres along with you Mr Thompson, to depart my house, immediately."

Sir Chester stepped forward. "I say Charles, it was an accident. I believe, sir, you are overreacting to a simple mishap."

"On the contrary, sir. Had the accident occurred to anyone else I would have agreed with you. But to single out the fiancée of my niece whom you have disgraced several times since you all arrived, gives me a different theory. And every right to react the way I am."

"This is preposterous," yelled Alexander. "This so-called lady thinks all the attention is on her. What do we want with this harlot?"

"Take those words back, Alexander. My fiancée will not be disgraced by you or anyone else."

Lucas placed himself in front of his brother as Alexander came towards him.

"You have to tell them, James. This was a silly accident." Alexander said with little conviction. The smirk on his face told all he did not care what anyone thought.

"Except I do not believe it was an accident. Had I not stood from my crouching position a second before you shot, I would have received a fatal injury. You were aiming at me. Why? Answer me that Alexander."

"This is ridiculous." He turned and walked away, throwing his arms into the air. "No one will believe this story."

"I must admit it sounds totally unbelievable." Sir Chester added.

"Sir Chester, it might if it was not for your son Oliver who believes and has declared my niece as unworthy of being part of the society of Scotland."

"Preposterous. I have never heard him speak so. Truly man, you are mistook."

"You may not have listened to his rants, but I can give you a list of names of others who have heard him."

"I can remain quiet no longer." Oliver came and stood in front of Elspeth. "You have no right to be part of our society. What your brother did, means you are nothing. You might as well have joined him in the act of murder. His blood flows through you after all."

Elspeth stood tall in front of him and her other accusers.

"You fall in your accusations, sir. My brother committed the crimes. Not I. He was my brother, yes, but I did not know what he was capable of doing."

"But the fruit does not fall far from the tree. Unless the bad fruit is removed." Oliver added in a menacing tone.

Her face grew hotter. "Why do you not accuse Alexander? He was a very close friend of my brother." She pointed her finger directly at him.

Alexander came and stood before her. "Might be so, harlot, but we do not share blood. Bad blood must be removed."

Her uncle came and stood in front of her, distancing Alexander from her. It did not stop Lucas who jumped in front of her uncle and with his fist hit Alexander in the face. He staggered but did not fall.

He looked at Lucas. "You will regret your actions, young pup."

"Enough. Pack your bags and the cart will escort you to the inn at Portree. The Godfreys may stay. The rest of you will go."

Many of the gentlemen began to speak at the same time. Her uncle could not put up with anymore. He was red faced with anger.

"Enough." He yelled. "Remove yourselves now."

One maid stepped forward to encourage the Godfreys to come in for tea.

Elspeth held James close to her. She was shaking. Lucas stood between them and the other gentlemen as they passed by and went inside. Lucas had his hands still in fists. She placed a hand on his back.

"Lucas, please take James to his room. I will summon the physician."

Lucas helped his brother limp in. Her uncle, Charles, came and stood next to her and he placed his protective arm around her.

"I am sorry, Charles. This is all my fault."

"Not another word my dear. This is solely on the shoulder of the ghastly Mr Alexander Thompson."

14

STRANGE MAIL

Within the hour the physician had arrived, and the men had gone. The doctor removed all the shards of rock and cleaned the bullet wound. It was not as bad as she had imagined and was glad that James was not badly hurt. She sat on the edge of James' bed holding his hand throughout the procedure. He sat up with cushions behind him. He would be well. He needed to rest for now and then he would be able to move around with the aid of a walking stick Charles had gotten out of the attic.

"I just am still having trouble to think a man of Alexander's standing would attempt to kill you. Surely, my imagination saw the evil. But I spoke in haste. Perhaps it was not there? I mean, could he want to do that to you?"

"He did. I have no doubt. He was aiming at me. I just spotted him as I got up. It happened very quickly but there can be no other reason for the shot to my leg. Had I not stood up I would be dead. I know you, my dear. You would rather see the good in someone than the bad. It is one of the wonders I love about you. I am afraid there is no good in him, no matter how hard you look. Your observation of evil was correct."

"But why you? I thought I was on the hunting list." She gave a big sigh and shook her head. "Thankfully, they are gone."

"Yes, but I do not think this is the end for his pursuit. They have no sense of good or evil or right and wrong. They believe themselves to be great men, above the laws the rest of us follow. I am worried that they will be angry and seek further damage due to the disgrace levelled against them. They deserved it but they will not see it in those terms. The older gentlemen have no part in your disgrace. Not directly, I am sure. I do not think they even realise what their sons are involved in. But they will be furious at the disgrace and may seek to embarrass us."

"What are we to do?"

"Lucas has sent some servants and isle folk to watch them until they leave Portree. We will be aware of their movements. For now, let us just rest up and wait until they are gone. Rest assured, my love. I will protect you. As will all of my family. This scratch will not slow me down."

"All of this is so strange. What could they possibly want or even achieve by killing you?"

"I can understand relatively easily because I have some added information."

"Then please enlighten me, for I see nothing to warrant your death. They want me gone but not you."

"They wanted me out of the way so they can get to you. They want to hurt you. You are the ultimate target."

She shook her head. "I am not sure I understand…they want me disgraced. That is all."

"My dearest, I have received a letter from Chalanor. It has only just arrived a day ago." He looked deeper into her eyes. "I think reading it might help you understand. I wanted to tell you when it arrived yesterday, however so much had been going on, I thought I would wait. You already felt intimidated by these men. But after the events of this afternoon, you should be aware. I promised that

I would keep nothing from you. Trust me. After our joy last night..."

"You wanted to protect me. I understand. Now what is in this letter?"

He reached into the drawer of the cupboard beside his bed, then handed her a letter. She immediately recognised Chalanor's writing and began to read it.

"All I ask is that you read it through to the end before you make any comment. In fact, read it out loud. It may help me understand it more. I can hardly believe its contents."

"Very well, James."

"*My dear friend James,*

I have continued to investigate the "club" that Freddie was a part of. It seems it was far more widespread than we first imagined. There appear to be many members across both Scottish, English, and Welsh society. It may even have spread to the continent.

I have confirmed both Oliver McIntyre and George Broderick are members. They have only been members for about three years. They came to join through a mutual friend of Freddie, an Alexander Thompson. Seems Thompson and Freddie started the club when they were at university. It also appears they were the ones who actively recruited the members. Most of the gatherings were in a country house in Devon. A house owned by both Freddie and Alexander.

Their secrets were safe. No one was aware of the things these men did while they visited the house. After Freddie died, Alexander continued to visit the property. My solicitor was able to find out that he owned the house outright. Seems the deal between Freddie and Alexander was, if one should die then the other would continue the club and inherit the property. But our understanding is that Freddie paid for it.

Some members of the town have done their own investigations after Freddie died and have brought several tragedies to light. Seems five female bodies were found buried under a Rowan tree near the house. No one knows their names. Some believed they could have been women of the night. There are those who are looking into the possibility and line of enquiry. Alexander however escaped to Scotland before this came to light. It is believed he purchased another property in Scotland, having sold the property in Devon. He has continued the club there. We know it is near Aberdeen.

All the authorities assume Alexander knows about the bodies. In part with what came to light at the house, after the sale. It would seem Alexander left in a hurry.

Torture equipment was found. Branding irons, a rack, and various other items. They would have caused significant pain if used on any human or animal. And they were used. Blood stains were evident on the items. We believe the items were used on the bodies found.

But the most troubling news is one of the bedrooms. Seems Alexander is infatuated with Elspeth. The walls were scattered with her name, drawn in blood and ink on the walls. There were drawings of her. A waterfall and scenes of them involved in sexual acts near the falls.

After the house was sold, an attempt to set it alight failed. I assume he may have been destroying the evidence after he had made the money on the sale.

It was very disturbing, and I write you now to put you on your guard. Alexander, it would seem, has plans to fulfil a long-held design to do with Elspeth whatever he damn well pleases. As you can imagine both Louisa and I are very anxious you prevent him getting anywhere near Elspeth. I know you love her so by all means protect her. Save her from a fate worse than death. He was stopped prior to this due to his friendship and business arrangements with Freddie. Now Freddie is gone, we feel sure he will attempt something against Elspeth. It is his heart's desire, however ghastly the desire might be.

We await any news you can share and pray you are all safe and well. Keep your eyes open for Alexander Thompson.

Your friend Chalanor.

. . .

*E*lspeth lowered the missive to her lap. She stared at James. "What can I say?"

"My dearest, there is nothing to say. This investigation has been going on since your brother died. Knowing what he had done to the maid and Lady Farraday, it was essential to see what else might lay in his background. We didn't want anything else to arise that could cause further embarrassment to you or the rest of society."

"But I had no idea."

"Of course, my love. Your honour is not in question. We wanted to make sure we understood all of what had happened. Unfortunately, a great many more things have come to light. It would seem your brother's actions were many and varied. I am sorry to have to tell you this."

"Will this never end? I am not sure I can take any more of his deeds. Everything I thought I knew about a beloved brother is destroyed. Now it is becoming worse if it is at all possible."

He took her hands in his. "This information changes nothing. You are still the sweet girl, now woman, you always have been. What it reveals is that some men in our society are beasts. They demand strange rituals and rights no man should claim. Dream terrible dreams and act on some of those horrid things. I just need you to be safe."

"So, if this is all true…" She lifted the letter. "Alexander wanted you dead so he could get at me."

"Yes."

"Yes? I was really in hope you would say no." She lifted the corner of her mouth, attempting a smile. It did not work as the sudden heat of rage ran through her.

"I am afraid so. With me dead and unable to protect you, he would have had a road direct to you. But he wants you and I do not think that getting him out of the house will stop him from trying to get you."

She shook her head and lowered her gaze to her feet. She mumbled. 'How' and 'Why'.

"This is again a secret your brother held. He might not even have known of Alexander's desire for you. But in his eyes, now your brother is gone, you are fair game. These men do not see the good in man, woman, or child. Freddie was not alone in the beastly things men can do. Alexander can do what your brother did and probably worse. But my love, not all men are like him."

"I am aware of the love you have for me. You want only the best for me. I know, deep in my heart how you feel. But could these men really believe in nothing good? In pure evil?"

"Yes, my dear. Some men do not love or have respect for women. To them, women are property to do with what they want. Do you understand? For some it is money they can get. For others prestige. Women are a means to an end. And it always ends in sorrow. For me it is love. I want to be with you for the rest of our lives."

"I love you also. I know your heart. I think I have always known it. I have no money or prestige. In fact, I have a great deal of damage, and I think most men would run away."

"Not me. I have always wanted to be with you. And now we will be. Always."

15

___

THINGS THAT GO BUMP IN THE NIGHT

That night Elspeth was again standing in front of her open window looking out over the loch. She was in the dark and enjoying the moonlight streaming through her window. James was well. She let out a deep sigh. He would be walking around in a day or so. He was lucky the wound was superficial. Then there were the revelations in Chalanor's letter. Her thoughts then skipped to her brother—what reasons were there for him to become the beast he was now remembered as? What a loss. What great sorrow.

Alexander also entered her thoughts. She did not want to think about him. They were not pleasant thoughts. Would he really want to do to her the same terrible things her brother had done to Alice and Lady Farraday? What other dastardly things could he think up? Even James suggested that Alexander could do worse.

She smiled at the moon, wishing she could be on its surface far, far away from all these terrible thoughts and deeds. She looked out over the loch again and spotted it. Men in a small rowing boat heading for 'the Lump' as she had seen before. This time they were coming from the right side of the loch and not a ship. She had no idea where they had come from as that part of the island was uninhabited.

Smuggling had been the last thought she expected to come to mind. But like the other night they were heading for the small beach and the cave she knew was there in the dark. Four men. Two rowing and one seated at each end of the boat.

The night was still and the occasional sound of the oar hitting the water could be heard.

What was going on?

They soon disappeared from view. She stood there waiting. But she could not say why she waited. Her hesitation was paid off as she spotted another rowboat on the loch but this time rowing to the landing below the house. This disturbed her.

Was she dreaming? Maybe it was her imagination dealing her with illusions. But she looked again and there they were. Three men. Not the same group she had first seen. This was another rowboat.

She went to her door, unlocked it, and went down the stairs. She knocked at her uncle's door.

"Elspeth. What have you seen?" Her uncle knew she would not have left her room unless it had been extremely important. She smiled at him.

"Yes uncle. I saw three men in a rowboat heading towards our landing on the beach."

"Three, you say? Very well, leave it with me. You go to James and stay with him until I give you the all clear."

No questions, no queries. Her uncle just acted. His trust in her was astonishing. So many men just disregarded anything a woman said, let alone act on her ideas or suspicions. She went straight to James' room. She gently knocked and called his name. The door opened and Lucas stood before her.

"Oh my, is he well? Please tell me he has not taken a turn for the worse."

"Calm yourself, Elspeth. I could not sleep and came to see how he was and found him unable to sleep also."

"Come in, my dearest. What is the trouble?"

"I too could not sleep and have been gazing out over the loch. I saw the smugglers again. And then just now saw a rowboat heading to our landing. I went and told Charles and he told me to come here."

The room was lit by one candle. But the curtains were open.

"Please Lucas, close the curtains. If there are men wandering around, I do not want them to see us or know where we are."

He moved to the windows and closed all the curtains.

She came and sat on the bed next to James.

"I cannot believe they may already be plotting to do me harm."

"Let us wait to hear what your uncle has discovered."

"But James, will he be safe? If they were prepared to kill you then surely, they are prepared to kill my uncle also."

"Yes, it is true. But he will send out the manservants to see what is taking place. Fear not. Let us wait."

Lucas was pacing at the end of the bed. Back and forth he went. She could tell there was something on his mind. But what?

"Elspeth, do you still plan to marry my brother?" he asked

"Yes Lucas. Nothing for me is changed. I loved your brother long ago and I know we are meant to be together."

"Then do it soon and return with us to our estate."

"You sound troubled, brother. What ails you?"

"These demons who dare to call themselves men, want to hurt us all. And more importantly Elspeth. We need to protect her." His voice was raspy and loud. Most unlike him.

"You are Lucas. You are here and I feel safe."

"For now, but I agree with James these men are unrelenting."

There came a knock at the door.

"Open the door. It is Charles." Came the voice from the other side of the door.

Lucas moved to the door and unlocked it. Charles came in and locked the door behind him.

"All is clear. No one is about. But I want Elspeth to stay here with you James."

"Very well. But what of Elspeth's honour?"

"You are both honourable and will marry in the next few days. So do not fret. Any suggestion of impropriety will be refuted. Under the circumstances, honour be damned. Now, let us return to our rooms Lucas and get some sleep. We have a wedding to arrange."

Lucas hesitated. But then he left with Charles.

"Alone at last." He said with a French accent. He grinned, hoping to place a smile on her troubled face.

She tried to smile but it did not work. "Very funny. But at least it will be so for the coming days. The sooner we are married the happier I will be." She laid down on the bed next to him. "Now sir, please lay back and go to sleep. I need you to regain your strength. I expect you will have a lot to do when we are married."

"Yes ma'am. I hear and obey."

"And James, just hold me and make me feel safe again."

He took her into his arms. She lay atop the covers which was probably a good idea. He drew her close to him.

"Are you sure you want to marry?" he whispered.

"Yes, James. From the moment you suggested the idea I wanted it. But what of you? Do you still want me?"

"With all my heart." He kissed her cheek.

They lay still a moment then Elspeth sat up and blew out the candle. She moved back into his arms.

"Where will we live?"

"In our estate home."

"With your father?"

"No. Father has already moved to the dowager house on the far side of the estate, near the village. He said the big house was getting too big for him and he also wanted me to run more of the estate management. Truth be told I think he found it difficult to be in the house after mother died. There are elements of her in every room."

"I never expected to be the mistress of my own home. All that I thought had gone for good. But I will cherish what your mother has done. I look forward to seeing it again."

"I am delighted that you will be my wife and that you will run Collace House."

"Is it not strange that all the time we have known each other, I have only been to your home once? I remember it being a very green place, the grounds, I mean."

"In the summer it is. At the foot of Mt Dunsinane and near the village of Collace, it was a wonderful place to grow up. I explored the area well as a child."

"What was your favourite place?"

"That is easy. The mount. There are old ruins up there and it is said that it was the castle of Macbeth. I can imagine Shakespeare sitting upon the hill and coming up with his story. It is such a majestic place."

They talked and talked about their future life and experiences. But sometime during the night they fell asleep.

16

CLEAR SKIES

The next two days were a rush. The priest from the village came to see them regarding the wedding. They decided to have the wedding in the garden. Security was the greatest concern and her uncle wanted to be sure there were all precautions made. The chapel in the village was small. Plans to build a bigger building had not yet come to pass though the villagers desired it.

"I think the garden is a wonderful idea. God is everywhere in a garden and it is one of our favourite places to be." Elspeth turned around looking at all the areas of the garden.

"Settled then. Here we will marry. Thank you, Reverend MacIntosh. We will see you tomorrow just before two o'clock. And you are most welcome to stay for a late lunch."

"I am delighted to perform this wedding. Two people who are truly in love. God will anoint your union. I will see you tomorrow. I will bring the church register with me for you both to sign." The priest bowed and took his leave.

James took her hand and drew her to the seat where they had spent many happy hours.

"Are you content, my dear?" He lifted her hand and kissed her fingers.

"Most definitely. All is in order and I cannot wait to have you by my side every moment."

"That sounds delightful. But we have been inseparable for some time already."

She laughed "Very true."

"The day after the wedding, I have arranged for a ship to take us via the northern part of Scotland to Dundee. It will take at least two weeks. I know it a slow route, but it was the best I could do. They have various stops on the way. It will be a very relaxing trip I should think. We will alight at Dundee and then a carriage ride to Collace House. I want us home as soon as possible. When things are safer, I would love to come back here and relax. I want to see the isle from your viewpoint. I am aware of how much you love it."

"Again, I cannot fault your arrangements. I will miss this place. Viewfield has been home to me. And she has welcomed me. I thought I would be here for some time. I still have not had a winter here."

"Well, the weather is getting colder. I want to take the northern route before it gets too cold to do so. In another month I would not recommend it. The weather can be harsh."

"Is it not strange that we are now talking about the weather?" She laughed and he joined her.

They watched as his brother made his way to them.

"Lucas, come and sit with us." She moved closer to him so that Lucas could sit down. He bowed to them and then sat on the grass in front of them.

"I just wanted to give you a report about the gentlemen. All left on a ship this morning that was heading to Port Glasgow on the Clyde. The servants saw everyone on the ship. So, none remain in Portree. Which is a good thing as the fishermen were not happy they were in the village. They agreed they should not be here but wanted them as far from the village and as soon as possible."

"Well said. It is done then. None will be here on the morrow. We can breathe easier and enjoy our special day. However, I will still have people on watch."

"I am delighted to welcome you to the family. I have never had a sister so I am excited now I will have you."

"Lucas, you know how to make me smile. This is a dream. A dream from which I do not want to wake up. Thank you both."

———

*E*lspeth breathed a sigh of relief. She was in her bed as a single lady for the last time. She had slept well and had pleasant dreams. Now she was to wed a man whom she had known a great deal of her life. He was not like her brother nor was he vain. He was well respected and loved her despite her not having a penny or prestige to her name. She had nothing to offer him but her love.

In her head she heard his word.

Do not say that again. You are a talented and intelligent woman who has fallen on hard times. It does not change who you are. You are loved and the greatest gift I could ever receive.

She smiled and rolled over and sat up. Her curtains were open, and she liked the light streaming in. Before the past few days, she had wanted the world to be blocked out. Now she welcomed each new day with open arms.

Today was Wednesday morning, the day she would marry. She stood in front of the window. Her wedding day. Her mother was not here to witness what she had always wanted. But she knew her mother would be happy.

It would be wonderful if Chalanor and Louisa were here, but she had to accept it could not happen. She could go and see her dear friends as soon as possible. Then she could share the joy they had together, and she now had with James.

There was a knock at her door. Delia opened it and she entered with a maid who had her breakfast on a tray, coming in behind her.

"Delia, what is this?"

"Breakfast in peace and quiet. You can have a restful morning. Then I will do your hair and you will be dressed in time for the wedding."

"This is unexpected. I thought Morag had come to wake me."

Delia had a distant look in her eyes. And a slight frown appeared upon her lips.

"No, Morag is busy, but I wanted you to have a special morning. If my brother and Louisa were here, I am sure they would be looking after you. And besides, have we not become good friends these past days?"

"We have indeed. Thank you for the kind thought."

"You should thank your future husband. He asked if I would stand up and be your bridesmaid. I do so with pleasure. And Lucas will be his best man. Here is a light but nourishing breakfast for you. He has thought of everything."

"He certainly has. And I am delighted at the arrangements. Come let us have breakfast together."

"You guessed my plan."

She ushered Delia to her table and chairs. The maid had set everything up. The tea was hot and the bread still warm. They joked and smiled and kept looking out the window at the weather, as the clouds rolled in and then rolled away. A more delightful morning could not be had.

This was a wonderful way to start a married life, a life she never thought would be hers.

"*I* will not tell her..." James paced back and forward running his fingers through his hair.

"But..."

"This is her wedding day as much as mine. Her life has been turned upside down since her brother died. I will not have this special day ruined by such news."

"Lucas, I understand your concern, but I agree with James."

"But Father, how can we go ahead? I am certain Alexander is close by. The servants are not sure he stayed on the ship. There are doubts. And now the body."

"Enough. I will not hear of it. Not one more word. I will tell her after we are on the ship and sailing for home. She will be my wife. I will not have this day spoiled." He stood there with his hands on his hips.

"I will see if some of the fishermen from Portree will help us encircle the house and property until we leave tomorrow."

"Thank you, Father. I am sure it will help." He came and placed his hand on his brother's shoulder. "I hear your concern, but I want her to have joy today. Please Lucas, do not tell her. Grant me this."

Lucas nodded. He was not happy, and James could see the frown upon his face, but this was too much for today. Even he wished he did not know.

"I will arrange for others to keep searching and for all caution to be taken. I will not tell her. But I want to be there when you do tell her. I think this will be hard news for her to hear. We must do all we can to support her."

"Very well. Tomorrow, when we are on the ship. Thank you, Lucas."

*D*elia had done her hair. She had almost duplicated the look she had at the day of Chalanor and Louisa's wedding. How could Delia know as she had not been at the wedding? She smiled. It was nice to be remembering the event as she prepared for her own wedding. Where had she gotten the artificial forget-me-nots, she had no idea. All she said was the flowers and fragrance James thought of when he was thinking about her, were forget-me-nots. She had given her a bottle of the fragrance. Of course, it was from her husband to be. James was doing all he could to make her feel wonderful.

It was fifteen minutes to two. She had seen the priest arrive about ten minutes ago. A few of her uncle's friends who lived in the area had also arrived with their families in tow. She watched as other people joined the procession up the hill.

Her stomach was doing little somersaults. Her dreams with James were about to begin. She smiled and wanted to shout for joy. They would finally live as husband and wife. This is what she wanted. This is what they both desired. A knock at the door brought her out of her reverie.

"Come in."

The door opened and her uncle entered.

"I am here to give you away, my dear. Something I am both glad and sad to do."

"Oh uncle. Things have not gone to plan, have they? I will no longer be your chatelaine."

"True, but I have gained a niece who will be happily married, and my sister would be proud knowing you will be happy rather than you staying with me."

She squeezed his hand. Her love for her uncle had grown so much in the time since her brother's death. He had been the first and only family member to come to her side and help her through the sale of the estate and everything else she had faced. He had offered her a home and she wanted to keep her distance and accepted the position of the chatelaine only. Now she was glad she had agreed to come. She had been reunited with a man she had loved a long time, even when she did not want to admit it.

She drew her uncle into a hug. She was sure he had helped to plan this reunion between her and James. Her mother had wanted her to marry James. Now she would give thanks to her dear uncle. And she would always be grateful.

"I wanted to give you something. Something special."

"There is no need, uncle. You have done so much for me already. Especially getting James to come."

"I promise you; it was not difficult to get him here. No, I want to give you something of your mother's."

"But uncle…"

"I gave her a Scottish pearl, hanging on a golden chain when she married your father."

"But uncle, I am sorry. It was one of the things sold in the estate sale."

"I am well aware of that, my dear. For I was the one who purchased it, a second time, you might say. So that I could give it to you today when you married."

He took it out of his pocket, and she turned around, so he could place it around her neck.

"It is now home, where it should be."

"You look beautiful. I am so very proud of you."

"I love you uncle. I will cherish it. Because it was for mother and me. Thank you and thank you for helping this come about."

"You are more than welcome my dear. Welcome into society yet again. We will do all in our power to make you feel welcome."

He placed his arm out towards her. "Now my dear, let me take you to your future husband."

There was a light breeze as she came through the doors from the dining room. James and Lucas were standing near the bench, a special place for her. The clouds had gone, and the sun was shining. This was what she had hoped, and the day did not disappoint.

She then came to stand before her James.

The priest began.

"Before we begin, I must address the reason we are not in the chapel. It is a very small building and the bride and groom wished to be close to home for the ceremony. I have the standard book of prayer; the words Christ would want to hear the couple speak. Let us begin. I know Christ is with us today.

Dearly beloved, we are gathered together here in the sight of God and in the face of this congregation...."

She looked into James' eyes. They glistened with unshed tears of what she hoped were pure joy. He squeezed her hand as the priest mentioned children might come from the union.

She shuddered at the word fornication. She could tell James had noticed. He began to rub her hand.

Then the priest said the words she did not want to hear.

".... these two persons present come now to be joined. Therefore, if any man can show just cause, why they might not lawfully be joined together, let him now speak, or else hereafter for ever hold his peace."

Elspeth exited the door from the dining room. She had dressed in a pale purple cotton and a dark purple short spencer made of velvet over her dress. She looked breathtaking. He had waited so long for this day to arrive. It had not been the way he had wanted it, in a great cathedral in England or Scotland, but she was happy they had chosen the garden. All he wanted was for her to be happy. He wanted to cry as she stood still and at peace in front of him. He squeezed her hand when the priest had mentioned children. He had wanted children but only with her. She was beautiful and would make beautiful children. He wanted to have some in the years to come. But now he wanted to concentrate on her and her happiness.

She gave a shiver on the word fornication. Her brother was still here in her thoughts. He wished it were not so, but he loved her all the more. Because she loved her brother despite his misdeeds.

Fear and colour crossed her face as the words he did not want to hear were said.

"...why they might not lawfully be joined together, let him now speak, or else hereafter for ever hold his peace."

He squeezed her hands again. Her eyes were closed, and he wished she would open them and see his determination and resolve to protect her. She did and beamed at him with a smile so beautiful.

He smiled, but almost cried with joy as the words from the priest continued to flow. No one had intervened. No one would spoil their day. He silently thanked God. He wanted her to enjoy this day.

The vows were exchanged, and Uncle Charles had stepped forward to give her away. Yes, he was his uncle now too. Extra words of blessing were given by the priest. Then the part he had waited for.

Lucas placed the golden band with the Celtic Knots engraved on its surface on the priest's prayer book.

"Repeat these words please; with this ring I thee wed,"

"With this ring I thee wed."

"With my body I thee worship."

"With my body I thee worship." He squeezed her hand again and her eyes glistened.

"And with all my worldly goods I thee endow;"

"And with all my worldly goods I thee endow;"

"*In the name of the Father, and of the son and of the Holy Ghost. Amen*"

"In the name of the Father, and of the son and of the Holy Ghost. Amen"

The priest then spoke to the congregation. He said a prayer and they were married. Others gathered around them. But he only had eyes for her, and he sensed it was the same for her. He leaned down and kissed his bride and was listening to the cheers of those around him as he picked up his wife and carried, her over the threshold, back into the dining room. They were married. At last.

17

OH, HAPPY WEDDING NIGHT

The dining room shone. White clothes decked all the tables. It made the room glow. The main family table had been moved over to allow two other tables to be placed in the room.

James placed her on her feet.

"I do hope Mrs Raeburn is happy with the decorations."

And she was. Walking through earlier she had not noticed the beauty of the room. She was so distracted to get to James.

"Where on earth did you get the beautiful roses?"

"Ah, your uncle had a word with his cousin in Armidale."

"They are delightful."

He escorted her to the family table and was greeted by her uncle.

"My dearest Elspeth, my joy abounds. I am so happy for you and James. You will be blissfully happy."

She hugged her uncle.

"I think we will be, Charles. There has been enough sadness in our lives. It is now time for joy."

"I could not agree more." James added and leaned over and kissed her on her cheek.

"Nor could I." added her father-in-law. She hugged him also. "I suddenly have a very large family again and it is wonderful." A tear slid down her face. He reached up and wiped it away. Gently persuaded by him, she sat in the seat at the table. He sat on her right and Delia sat on her left. Delia was beaming. She took her hand.

"I am overjoyed for you and James. I hope one day I can experience such joy as I see in you both."

"Thank you, Delia. And thank you for being a special part of our special day."

———

The remainder of the day was wonderful. They ate such beautiful food. No expense was spared. She knew the servants had been busy in preparation, but she could see half the isle must have been involved, explaining the many visitors to View-field. They came and went all day, some ladened with food and others with gifts. The clouds rolled in again but to her the sun was shining. A day of sunshine and joy.

The meal started with a tasty ham and pea soup. The clouds had come in again. Candles had been lit. The soup reflected the light. She breathed in the strong scent of the ham and the fresh garden peas. She had not tasted anything so delightful. It was autumn and the soup was the perfect start to an extended meal.

Then venison with vegetables and baked onions were presented. James carved the meat at their table and the servants served all the guests. There was also a small serving of a vegetable pie. It was pre-cut and the maids were delivering to all who sat at the tables. Even to those who were in the garden outside.

She was sure she could not eat another bite. But when the cook

Mrs McDougal and some of the villagers came out with dishes and dishes of baked apples, she had to think again. The smell of cinnamon hung in the air as servings were given to them and all the guests. A feast the likes of which had not been seen on the isle for many a year. Through all these events she watched James who continued to have eyes only for her. His smile never left his face.

After the meal, the tables were removed, and chairs were placed around the outer edges of the room. A string quartet entered and set themselves up in a corner. As they began to play, couples went to the centre of the room and began to dance. Soon the room was abuzz with dancing, singing and merriment. For some hours they enjoyed the dancing and singing old island tunes and Scottish melodies. They laughed and sang as the shadows became longer and the sky darker.

She went around to all the guests and thanked them for coming or doing any of the preparation. Her earlier thought of half the isle being involved proved to be right. So many of her uncle's friends had done what they could to make the day a roaring success. For someone who had been rejected by the London *ton*, she knew what it was to be loved and cared for by the isle inhabitants. They had accepted her without reservation.

Supper was served as the evening became dark. Mrs McDougal outdid herself again. Little strawberry tartlets must have used up every jar of preserved strawberries of the summer. Gingerbread biscuits and a bucket load of tea. Also, little apricot cakes. And for those who did not have a sweet tooth, cheese tartlets and baked cheesecakes were available. Finally, plain grained bread and cheese were served. This feast would be talked about for years to come.

Elspeth had come to the open door of the dining room to look at the final bit of light disappearing from a day that she would never forget.

"May I have a penny for your thoughts?"

James placed his arm around her waist and whispered thank you in her ears. She held him in her arms.

"I have never been so loved." He held her closer. He loved her. "I am contemplating what a wonderful day we have had."

He leaned in and whispered, "And our night is yet to come."

She turned to look into his eyes. She lifted her hand to his cheek and cupped it. "Oh yes. I have not forgotten. The best is yet to come."

"Rest assured, it is. And I plan to do to you all the wonderful things I promised. Now and evermore."

"Then perhaps it is time for us to say goodnight." She placed a kiss on his nose, and they entered the room again. Before long, they had left the party below and gone to her room. Their bridal suite for the evening. A beautiful September evening she would never forget.

---

*H*e drew her into her room knowing she was to be surprised with what he had arranged. The candles were lit and the roses which had been on the dining tables earlier were placed all around the room. One of the servants had taken some of the roses and removed the petals and scattered the petals on the bed.

"Oh James. How beautiful."

"As beautiful as you, Elspeth. I love you more than you will ever know. Thank you for becoming my wife."

She looked into his eyes and gentle tears fell from her eyes.

"Tears of joy my love. Tears of joy." She nodded.

He took her into his arms and kissed her lips. He deepened the kiss and lavished her lips with his mouth and tongue. Moments passed but finally he pulled away from her, turned and locked the door.

"Now it is just us, my love. I want to slowly undress you and make love to the only woman I have ever loved. I want you to feel everything. From the top of your head to the tips of your toes. I am yours forever and I plan to love you forever."

He reached up and undid the pearl necklace hanging around her neck. Her short spencer had been removed during the night's festivities as she became hot. He turned her around and slowly undid the buttons on her dress, while placing kisses on her neck. She leaned back into him on occasion rather more interested in the kissing than having her dress removed.

After distracting lips and caresses, her dress lay at her feet. Her slip was the only thing that lay between him and her body. He started to shift his hand to her shoulder. But she stopped him. She kicked off her slippers and her stockings.

"Now, let me oblige you with your clothes being removed, by me." She lifted her hands and undid his cravat. He took pleasure in watching her eyes widen as she opened the buttons at the top of his shirt. He whipped the shirt off over his head. She placed her hands on his chest and he thought the heat from her hands would make him explode at any moment. Her hands were warm and caressed him. But the heat made him want to throw her to the bed and devour her. He sat on the edge of the bed and removed his own boots. This was not an easy task, but she watched him none the less. He noted the cheeky smile upon her face. The temperature in him lowered.

He stood there in his britches and she in her slip.

"Is what you see acceptable?"

"Oh, my dear James, I have dreamed of this moment. Please take me completely and make me your wife and not just in name."

An invitation that he could not refuse. He took her hand and drew her to him. He lifted her and placed her on the bed. His hand reached up to the apex of her body. He placed his fingers gently on her sensitive spot and began to rub. Her moans of pleasure enticed him on. He reached up and moved her slip towards her head. In one quick movement she removed it and there she was. Naked and beautiful in front of him. Her legs were slightly apart, and his hand still caressed her.

He removed his hand and then removed his britches. He stood naked before her, giving her time to see him.

"I have seen my brother naked once. And did not comprehend what the male figure was, for me or any other woman. But now I know I want you inside of me more than I have wanted anything in my life."

He came to her and gently rubbed his penis on her moist place. He kissed her neck and her breast until she could not bear it any longer.

"James, come inside me please."

And he did. He pressed against her virginity until it gave. IIe stopped to allow her to understand what he had done and take the volume of him. Then slowly he rocked back and forward. Soon she had joined in the dance. They knew each other completely and finally his secd spilled inside her. Her cries of joy echoed in his mouth. He did not move but allowed the blood thumping around him to reach into his very heart. Never had he been so complete. He slumped to her side and drew her close to him.

"I love you, Elspeth."

"I love you, James."

The night drew in around them and they slept a while. But this was a night of joy for them both. And they would share the pleasure of each other many more times. This was just the beginning, of everything.

18

LEAVING

Elspeth was standing at her window looking out over the loch. He came up behind her and wrapped his arms around her.

"Are you happy, my dearest?"

"Yes James." She placed her arms over his.

"Contemplative?"

"Yes. This is not where I expected my life to be. I thought I would be here on the isle for the rest of my life. Do not mistake me. I am overjoyed we have come together. It is just not what I expected."

"I want you to be happy. To be the person you want to be."

"I imagine for a while I will have to adjust my outlook until I can determine what I can do. I know I will be your wife and I hope we will be blessed by one day having children. But I want to be more than those things. I want to be your helper in many ways."

"Once we are home and you make the place feel like your home as well as mine, I am sure your mind will find the places you want to be. Just talk with me. Share your concerns. Share all. I plan to do the same. I have things I want to tell you and share with you but after we leave here. Together we can be so much more than either of us imagined. We are starting a new life, together."

"My things are packed. I have discussed with Charles and asked if this room be left for us. He is delighted to do so. To know things my mother loved, and I adored, will be here, makes me happy. I hope we can come to rest here often. I really do love this isle."

"I am sure we will, my dear. Elspeth, this will always be a place special in my heart. It is where we found each other again."

"Yes, we have." She looked around smiling and thinking. "I have packed my telescope. I hope to set it up somewhere in the house."

"Our bedroom looks out over the fields to the Firth of Tay. It is not as close as you are here, but you can watch the ships again. It's only about 5 miles away as the crow flies."

He turned her around and gave her a gentle kiss on her lips.

"What is it you need to tell me?" she asked, looking into the grey blue pools of his eyes.

"Ahh. Would you do me the honour of waiting till we are on the boat?" He gave her a cuddle.

"I feel that my husband is protecting me again."

"Perhaps but I want to look after you. I will never keep anything from you for long. You know me. May I continue to protect you?"

"Yes, my dear. You may."

They left her room, which was now theirs and headed down to the landing.

*U*ncle Charles was waiting for them. He took her into his arms and held her close.

"I will stay another week and then return to my estate near Perth. We are but twenty miles away as the crow flies. I hope I will see you often. I promise once I have seen to my estate, I will come to visit you both."

She swallowed but could not. Something thick was in her throat. Tears were flowing down her cheeks and no sound came from her mouth. James squeezed her hand and answered for them both.

"We also hope to see you often, Charles. And we look forward to seeing you in a few weeks or so. Can I thank you for letting me know Elspeth was coming?"

Elspeth smiled at her uncle as the tears continued down her cheeks.

"No need for tears, my dearest girl. You are reunited with your love and I for one could not be happier."

"These are both tears of joy and sadness if it is possible." She choked out amid the tears.

"It is, Elspeth. I will see you again very soon."

James helped her into the dinghy then turned and shook his new uncle's hand. He got into the boat just as they were pushing it out.

He sat down next to her and took her hand. She waved at her uncle with the other hand and cuddled in closer to her James.

Life will be so different and so wonderful.

---

*D*elia, Lucas, and James' father were already on the ship, a wooden clipper and helped the couple onto the deck. The sails were set, and the ship made its way out of the loch and into the Sound of Raasay. They headed North. The scenes of the isle to their left were breathtaking. She had come to the isle overland and had then taken a smaller boat across from the mainland to Portree. To see her beautiful isle from this unique viewpoint was beyond what she had imagined. Especially when they passed kilt rock. A finer name they could not have bestowed. Breathtaking were her thoughts. Breathtaking was her view.

James took her to the poop deck and sat her on a barrel strapped to the side rails. He lifted her with ease. Oh, how he cared and showed his concern for her comfort and wellbeing.

"I said I would tell you everything and I shall. But I wanted you to know I have kept something from you. Not to hurt you or because I don't trust you."

Her father-in-law, Delia and Lucas joined them on the deck. They stayed close.

"James, what is it?"

"Please understand I wanted nothing to spoil our beautiful day."

"And nothing did, and I am forever grateful. It was the most wonderful day of my life. But please do not concern yourself. I know your heart and you are telling me what I need to know, now."

"Very well. A lot occurred before we wed. It seems from our investigations; Morag was having an affair with Alexander."

"Morag? What has happened? I did not see her to say goodbye. I thought she must have been working at the beaches." She paused looking at the sombre faces around her. "But you have more to say. This will not be pleasant news, will it?" She did not expect an answer. It was bad.

Dreading what James would tell her, she bowed her head.

"The day before we married, her body was found on the beach near the smugglers cave. She had been brutally beaten and tortured. I am sorry to say this, but Alexander did all he could to hurt her in as many ways as he could."

Looking into her lover's eyes, she could see his pain. This was something he did not want to share with her, and she understood why. But he was keeping his promise of always keeping her informed with events and information. The tears were welling up inside her and she so wanted to scream. Tears filled her eyes and flowed freely.

Suddenly her body was wracked with pain. Bending over she began to sob. First her brother's revelations and all he had done.

Life had changed for her forever. Now Alexander doing the same terrible things to one of the maids she knew. She could not stop weeping. Sobbing until she could cry no more. Everything her brother had inflicted on others came back. How could they do these things? How could men become such beasts? James held her during all the time she cried. She had no choice. She had to weep. They had long passed the isle when she lifted her head to look into his grey blue eyes again.

"I am sorry."

"Never apologise for your heart's pain. I wish I could have kept it from you. We doubled all the sentries for the wedding as we knew then Alexander had not left the isle. But we are heading home. A new home for you where I will do all I can to protect you."

"Yes…" She remained quiet as she fathomed the information. She could see the concern on James' face. But also, on the faces of Delia, Lucas, and her father-in-law. She wanted to come up with ideas to protect them as much as herself. For their relationship with her put them all in danger.

"How can we get rid of him completely? Even if he is cornered, he does not appear to be the kind of man who will not fight till the end. How many others have to die or be wounded till he is stopped?" The pain raked her body to utter these words. She did not want them to be true. But they were.

"I do understand. You will always think of others before yourself. But my concern is for you. We know that it was he who murdered Morag. She had her suspicions so left a letter in her room, addressed to you as a matter of fact. She predicted what he could do. Do you wish to read it?"

She nodded and he reached into his coat pocket and handed her the missive.

She opened it.

It read:

. . .

Dear Miss Elspeth

I have been a foolish girl. All your warnings to me to keep away from the gentlemen, I ignored. I was sure Mr Thompson had real feelings for me. Making love to him was one of the most exciting things I have ever experienced. But he used me. I know now. He asked many questions about you. At first, I did not answer but then he became violent. I tried to keep away from him, but I loved what he did to me and how he made me feel when he did not hit me. I hope you understand. I needed him.

The day Mr James was wounded, I knew in my heart he had done it. Alexander. I confronted him and he hit me, telling me to keep quiet. He would not let me go back to my room. He apologised when he saw my fear and asked me to meet him on the beach tonight and he would make it up to me.

I agreed knowing he was leaving the isle in the coming days. I wanted to enjoy him as long as I could.

But miss I became concerned he might not leave. I am writing this letter, because I am concerned he may hurt me so badly I can't let you know or warn you. So, my confession is here and if I should die it will be at the hands of Mr Alexander Thompson. I do not trust him anymore. But I will try to stop him by promising myself to him.

Please forgive me ma'am. And I hope you and Mr James will be very happy together. I hope I will be back to see you wed.

Your faithful servant,

Morag

She lowered the letter and silent tears ran down her cheeks. She could not sob anymore. She could not shed more tears. This pained her, as she had shed so many. Could she not shed some more for Morag? Bewildered and confused, she knew there was more to this. She needed to hear what else they knew. There had to be more.

She looked at James.

"Now tell me. I know that there must be more than just this."

"Yes, there is more. It will disturb you to hear it."

"It might but nothing can be worse than the loss of Morag. Tell me what more you know?"

"Very well. When we found her body, we searched the area. We went into the cave and found two more girls from the village, who had been tortured like Morag had. One dead and the other barely alive."

She could not lift her head. "What did he do to them? I need to know what he is capable of. After all they died instead of me."

Lucas and Delia came to stand with her. Both placed a hand on her back. Their love and concern surrounded her.

"It will not be enlightening as much as frightening." Lucas added.

"But I need to know. What is he capable of?"

"I will tell you, my dear. Morag was raped many times. We do not know if he had other men with him, but we believe he did. She was beaten. She was branded with an FA. We believe that stands for…"

"Freddie and Alex perchance? Go on." Her head was still bowed.

"He also had her tied up, as rope marks were around her hands and feet. And he cut her and the others."

"Cut as in used a knife? He actually cut them?" She was looking into his eyes. His eyes were filled with pain.

"Yes."

She lowered her head again thinking.

Surely, they could do something to stop this man?

"With the letter and the evidence of the bodies and what was found in the cave, can we not have him brought to justice?"

"Yes, we plan to do that. All the information and details of what he did have been sent to the Magistrates in Edinburgh. The girl who is still alive will give evidence. She is being well protected and will eventually be taken to Edinburgh. But he will need to be found if he is to be convicted."

"I am still in danger?"

"Yes, my dear. He still has plans for you. Morag was but a diversion."

She stood. "James, can we go to our cabin. I wish to rest and think about what I now know."

"Thank you, Lucas, Delia and dear Raeburn. I just wish to be alone a while. I hope you will understand."

James offered his arm, and she placed her hand on it and they went to their cabin.

The following days on board were not as rough as he had expected. His Elspeth stayed in the cabin most of the time. She came to eat with the rest of the passengers but headed back to their cabin almost immediately after each meal. She needed to think, to process all she had heard. He understood that and wanted her to do so. He also wanted her to come to terms with a chapter in her life that she thought was over.

His father was concerned for her wellbeing. He came to see her often and offer her all he had to help her understand. As was Delia and Lucas who also spent time with her. But she wanted to think most of the time and asked them to be patient. It was a slow voyage but, in some respects, he knew she appreciated that it was. Allowing her the time to think had been useful. Just over two weeks and now they were near home.

On the last night she went onto the deck and he followed. He had been careful to give her the space she needed but he never left her out of his sight.

"We will be docking in Dundee tonight and will go ashore in the morning."

"It will be nice to be on land again, but I am concerned. Has Alexander followed us? Either by land or sea? Will he start to make things difficult for me?'

"Please do not disturb yourself. We will have protection and once he is caught, he will be sent to Edinburgh and will face the consequences for his actions. Trust me. He will be caught."

"I trust you. I just do not trust him."

"I love you, dearest."

"And I love you James, with all my heart."

Finally, the boat docked at Dundee during the evening. She was having trouble sleeping. He was careful not to say anything. They went on deck early in the morning while it was still dark. James did not leave her side.

"I will hold you in my arms forever, if it will give you peace."

"I will be at peace my dear, when he is caught and taken away. I will be happier when we are home, and I can feel normal again. But being in your arms forever is tempting."

"I love that you call Collace home."

"It will be my home because you will be there. You are home for me."

He held her close. He rejoiced at her description of home. He wanted to be that and more. He wanted comfort for her but with the bastard Alexander roaming the world, he knew in his heart she would be restless. He understood and would do for her what he could. If only when they arrived at Collace House, word will arrive telling them he had been found. He hugged her closer. Then he tried to distract her.

"In the morning, our carriage will be there awaiting to take us home. I have arranged for you to have a maid and for suppliers from Edinburgh to come and see you over the coming weeks. You see I wrote many letters before we wed."

"James, you are always thinking of me. Thank you. I hope there will be word the mad man has been captured. I also want letters from Chalanor and Louisa. They may have found out more. Please understand my love, I want this negative part of my life to end. I have had enough of it. We can then build a beautiful future together. Does that make sense?"

"It does, my Els."

"Oh, James you haven't called me Els since, since…"

"Since we were children. I loved calling you Els. May I?"

"Of course, my darling. Now let us lie on our bunks and wait for the morning." She took his hand, and they went below. And for the first time in some days, he sensed she had turned a corner and could see the light. The light of their future. He could see a glint of light in her eyes. For weeks her eyes had been dulled and turned into herself. Now she was looking forward. That lit her eyes. The future. And he wanted to head straight for it.

19
___

COMING HOME

They disembarked around nine in the morning. The salty air was refreshing as a light breeze blew across the mouth of the Firth of Tay. It was cool. After all, it was late September and winter was slowly making its way towards them. They stopped at the inn and had a light breakfast. By then the cart had been loaded with the luggage from the boat. Lucas left with the cart and began the trip home. Raeburn, Delia, James, and Elspeth went in the carriage. Delia had promised to stay a while and he had asked her to help Elspeth to relax and settle in. Lord Farraday went to see Delia's aunt to discuss what Delia wanted to do and would stay in Scotland for a while. He would come to Collace House in a week or so.

The ride was pleasant enough. It was fifteen miles to the house and another mile beyond for his father. They stopped at Knapp which was around ten miles from Dundee to rest the horses and themselves. There were only a few houses and the coach inn. It was connected to an adjoining estate but on the coach route to Dundee and to Perth.

All were in good spirits despite the weather beginning to turn.

Rain began about half an hour before they got home. He noted as the weather changed so did Elspeth. She became quieter and even more tentative. He did not know what to say or do for her. If he could take her fear, he would. Her eyes told him that she feared almost everyone around her. This Elspeth was not the girl he had fallen in love with so long ago. But it was part of her now, after all the dark experiences in her life. He would always love her, but he wanted to see less of this part of Elspeth for her sake as well as his.

____

It was early afternoon when the carriage pulled up in front of the house. She really could not remember much of the building from her last visit. That was a lifetime ago. She looked out of the window of the carriage at a mammoth four storey house. The stairs led to the first floor bypassing the ground floor that was probably the servant areas and the kitchens. It was made from red sandstone. It was rugged and almost castle like in its appearance.

But it had many windows which she knew would allow a lot of light to enter the building. And since James had re-entered her life, she wanted the light. She needed it.

The weather had turned grey and she knew she had too. Still thinking about if Alexander would seek her out. That was what troubled her. She knew James was worried. He barely let go of her hand. And he was constantly looking at her with expressions of concern written all over his face. She marvelled at the way she had slipped back into knowing him so easily. And she did know him. She could determine his moods and his feelings at a glance. She might not be able to read others, but she could always read him. And it was reassuring. She had no desire to manipulate him, but she did want to know him better. Marriage was getting to know each other better. More intimately as well as of the mind.

She continued to gaze out the coach's windows. The gardens were not as green as she remembered, and trees were showing their rusty colours. Autumn was in its zenith. She was seeing the house in a different time. Now it was to be her home. She had always liked autumn but in the south of England. Here it was already very cold, and the colours seemed stronger than the colours of southern England. With an almost constant grey sky she was feeling low despite the beauty surrounding her.

The butler brought out an umbrella and took her into the house up the main stairs. He did not hurry her but took his time allowing her to take her own pace. She looked over the railing and saw there was a sunken floor below the ground floor. She gave up wondering how many floors the house had. The butler went back for Delia.

She was in the foyer and a maid was helping her take off her coat, as Delia and James arrived. All the staff were there in a semi-circle to greet her. She smiled and reached out her hand to James, so he could take her around and start the introductions.

———

He took her hand and noticed she was shaking. He placed his arm around her waist and drew her in close. She in turn placed her arm around him. The poor dear was terrified.

The butler came to stand next to him.

"Walker, may I introduce you to my wife and your new mistress, Elspeth Raeburn."

"Ma'am." He bowed to her.

She smiled. "Thank you, Walker. Would you be so kind as to introduce everyone else to me?"

"Certainly, ma'am." Walker came and stood beside her as she made her way around the circle.

He followed, greeting his servants as well. He watched her and despite her fear, she easily had taken to the introductions. She was scared but the servants did not know it.

"This ma'am, is Lottie. She will be your private maid. She will be able to help you with anything related to your wellbeing and the house ma'am."

Lottie gave a curtsy. "I am proficient in hair design and also in writing letters, madam. I will do all I can to help you."

She had a Scottish lilt but had obviously spent time in London. She was not too tall and was slender. She had jet black hair, which she had arranged in a neat bun on the back of her head. She was new to the estate, but she would suit Elspeth. He cannot believe that he arranged for her to be hired before he had even gone to Skye. He hoped Elspeth would say yes but really had no guarantees but had hired Lottie anyway.

"Thank you, Lottie. Can you make sure my belongings are taken to the main bedroom, please?"

"Yes madam."

He could see the strange look which quickly crossed the maid's face. Please and thank you were words not often used with servants. Well, that would change. He knew Elspeth. She would thank them.

After all she knew what it was like to be a servant.

"And this ma'am, is the cook Mrs McKibben."

"A pleasure to meet you Mrs McKibben. James says you make the greatest potato cakes in Scotland."

"Master James spoils me, mistress. But I do think they are rather good." Mrs K as he called her, grinned at him.

Her accent was thick, but she was polite and had a big smile across her face. She was in her fifties. She was rounded but not fat. Elspeth and she would get on, he had no doubt.

"I am sure you have the meals planned for the next few days, but could we meet in the morning after breakfast and you can give me a tour of your kitchen and tell me how you do things here."

"But of course, mistress. I will be delighted." And a big smile was on Mrs K's face and remained there and Elspeth in turn breathed a sigh of relief. He felt it as he came and placed his arm around her again.

He whispered, "Well done, my dear."

And so, they went on down the line. She met everyone including the gardeners.

"Now sir and ma'am, if you would like to come to the day room, we will fetch your tea." Walker used his left hand to direct his mistress to the day room.

"I would like to wash up first but will join you in ten minutes."

Lottie was by her side in a second.

"May I escort you to your dressing room, madam?"

"Yes, thank you Lottie."

He lifted her hand to his lips and kissed her fingers.

"We will see you shortly, my dearest."

She almost floated up the stairs. She seemed more relaxed again. Her emotions were truly going up and down. She will survive this. She must.

---

*L*ottie prepared water for her to wash and then left her alone. She looked out the window which was at the front far right on the second floor. She thought for a moment. Yes, if she was looking at the house it was the far right. James and her bedroom were next door, and his dressing room was on the other side of the bedroom, closest to the stairs.

James did not lie. The view to the Firth of Tay from the window was remarkable. It was cloudy but she could see the Firth clearly. She looked forward to seeing it on a clear day.

She did her ablutions and readied herself to go downstairs. Lottie knocked and came in.

"Is there anything else I can do for you, madam?"

"No thank you, Lottie. I will head down to the day room." She paused. "Actually, I don't know where the day room is. Can you escort me?"

"But of course, madam. Please follow me."

And Elspeth did.

<hr>

They had made love and were holding each other. The curtains were open, and she was thinking how she hated having the curtain open just a month ago. But James had helped her change in many good ways. The most important, she needed him, and he needed her.

"Are you happy Els?"

"I am. Tired, happy, content and in love. What a great combination."

"Sounds wonderful to me. You have had a few very busy and life changing weeks. I just want to be sure all is well with you."

"I promise I will tell you if there is something amiss. When I am with you, I am fine. Has mail come from Chalanor?"

"Yes, but I have not opened any of the mail. I thought you could join me on the 1st floor tomorrow after you tour the kitchen with Mrs K."

"Oh, so that is the name you have for her?"

"Yes. She started in the kitchens when she was around twelve but was well before I was born. Then about twenty years ago she became the head cook. And your comment about her potato cakes will make you shine in her eyes."

"I do not plan to change anything as yet. If things are running smoothly then I wish to keep it running smoothly."

"But this is your home, and the staff are well aware you are the new mistress. You may do what pleases you."

"Watching and learning from them will be my start. They know more about this house than I do."

"You are very good, my dear. Now will you join me tomorrow?"

"Yes James."

"And Elspeth, if being near you keeps a smile on your face, I will never leave your side."

20

LET THE NEW LIFE BEGIN

The sun was up when she opened her eyes. James was still asleep, cuddled up next to her. She listened to his deep breathing. Never could she believe she would find love like this. Everything about James excited and also calmed her. What a juxta-position. She closed her eyes and listened again to his calming breath.

She heard a tapping at the door.

"Enter Lottie."

"It is Jasper, ma'am. His lordship asked me to bring you tea."

Jasper was James' manservant. He helped him in his office and with his wardrobe. They seemed more like friends than master and servant. James had confirmed it was same for him also. Lottie came in and placed the tray with the teapot and cups on the table near the window. The window with the curtains open. James stirred and sat up.

"Thank you, Jasper and Lottie." Saying thank you was the step forward he would take to follow her example and support her. They curtsied and left the room. He got up and put on his dressing gown and then got hers from the end of the bed and helped her to put it on.

"Come, let us have tea."

They sat in front of the window. The morning light pouring into the room.

"We can start the day like this each day, if you like?"

"I would love to do just that."

"It's eight now. Breakfast will be at eight-thirty. My day starts around nine with the estate steward or as the Scots say, Gilly. But I would love to not rush the day and spend what I can with you. I am married, you see? And I love my wife."

"Oh James, I love you too. And yes, I would adore to start our day as you described it. Sitting here and discussing what we will do."

"Then Lady Raeburn, we will." he paused and smiled. "My father will be delighted to hear you being called Lady Raeburn, as am I. Will you join me in my study after your tour of the kitchen? I can then walk with you through the whole house and describe where everything is."

"Yes, my dear. After my kitchen tour I will arrange to have tea brought to your study. Then if it suits you, can we check the mail first? Before we tour the house?"

"Of course, my darling, I will have the letters waiting for you."

"Thank you. I am sorry I am distracted. But I am keen to see if Chalanor has found out any more information."

"I understand and I want you to be comfortable. I will do whatever you want to make you feel safe."

"I know, my love."

"Now let us have our tea." And he poured her a cup.

Mrs K was a wizard. She was one of the most organised cooks she had ever met. Her kitchen was spotless, and her staff practiced the same. Everything had a place and she had great produce from the tenant farmers and the local area. This woman knew her job. There was no way she would interfere. She would suggest some recipes but only of things she might like to try. And she could not wait to try many of Mrs K's meals. Potato cakes had already been part of the breakfast menu. Delia was loving the change. Delia looked happier now she was back on the mainland. Lucas had already arranged to take her on a tour of the estate while she and James were busy. She also planned to write many letters. But a smile seemed to be constantly on her face.

The kitchen was on the sunken floor. Along with an icehouse and food storage areas. Mrs K also had a room or study where she prepared the menus and ordered the food. The staff called the whole area the underground. There were also two rooms where the kitchen staff slept.

The ground floor had many offices and space for staff to do preparations for dinners and functions. Items not used all the time were also stored here. It had cleaning materials and an office for the butler. He could see directly down the driveway. He had a quick access area which had stairs, leading to the front door where he would magically appear when a coach made its appearance. The Gilly also had an office on this floor. Here he would meet with the Laird and discuss many of the important aspects of the land and its uses. Nicklemas decorations, linen and all sorts were stored here. As Nicklemas was approaching, she asked Walker if she could have some time with him and some staff to sort out what they had. She hoped to make some new pieces to add to the estate collection. Leaving her touch.

The house itself was around one hundred years old, but to her, was one of the most modern stately homes she had ever seen. Everything had been thought out to the last inch of the building. She learned from Mrs K it was built by the 8th Lord Raeburn in 1717. It was considered a marvel then and really had not dated. A more modern home could not be found in the area, perhaps in all of Scotland. James' father was the 10th Lord Raeburn and was preparing to stand down to allow James to be the 11th Lord. And with him she would be the lady of this great family and house.

This great house and all the history fascinated her, and she looked forward to spending time in the library, on the 1st floor, and discovering more about the ancestors of James.

She arranged for morning tea and Mrs K escorted her to James' study. She had enjoyed every moment and thanked Mrs K for the wonderful time and education in the house she had given this fine morning.

As she got to the door of James' study, she found Lucas waiting for her. She farewelled Mrs K and turned to face Lucas.

"Elspeth, dear sister. I was wondering if I could spend some time with you this afternoon. I need to tell you some things and I would rather tell you before I bring it to my brother's attention."

"Certainly, Lucas. But you do sound mysterious."

"I guess I am being, mysterious as you say, but it is important, and I do promise to tell you all."

"Shall we say three o'clock this afternoon?"

"Definitely. Meet me at the stables. There are a number of horses you could use if you wish to ride."

"I am not a good horsewoman. But I will be happy to meet the horses. I will meet you there at three."

He bowed.

"Thank you, Elspeth. I will see you at luncheon and then at three." He went past her and left her outside the door. What did he have to say requiring him to make a special time to see her?

There was a knock at the door. "Come." He called. "Elspeth, my dear. You do not need to knock. This is your home, and you can come into any room any time you wish."

"I assume that it is a habit that I gained as my uncle's chatelaine."

"Well, it is a habit I hope you will break."

He came over to her and took her in his arms and they kissed. A slow tasty morsel of what they share together, and he was immediately aroused. He deepened the kiss, and she did not resist. He could do this all day and he wanted to. But he thought their tea would arrive any moment and he was correct.

The knock at the door disturbed them.

"Come."

He continued to hold her in his arms. And rested his head on her forehead.

"Excuse me, my Lord and Lady."

"No need to apologise, Walker. I can tell you I am sorrier than you."

"Your tea."

"Please bring it in, Walker." she added.

He whispered in her ear. "Please my dear, do not move. I am quite aroused, and I would not like the servants to see."

She chuckled, kissed his nose, and turned around, making sure she still stood close to him and covering the important parts of his anatomy. He wrapped his arms around her.

Two maids brought the tea and some biscuits and placed them on the master's desk, curtsied then left. Walker bowed then closed the door.

"Thank you, my love, for saving my dignity."

"My pleasure." She reached down with her hand and rubbed his trousers in just the right spot.

He groaned, took her into his arms again and kissed her passionately.

"Do you want to go to our room?"

"I think we will really have the staff talking, don't you think?"

"Probably but we are newly married and can be forgiven."

He kissed her again and this time she pulled away.

"What say we get done what we need to, and we go to bed early tonight?"

"Promise?"

"Most definitely."

She went to the desk and poured them both a tea.

"How was your tour of the kitchen?"

"Oh James, it was marvellous. Mrs K is a sensation. I am so happy you have her. She is a delight and from what I can see a fantastic cook. She whipped up these biscuits as we were talking. Feel them they are still warm."

"I am just delighted to see you so happy. Now let us look at the mail. There are three letters from Chalanor. I opened them to place them in order but have not read them. Do you wish me to read them aloud?"

"I think it best. Besides, I like to listen to your voice." She sat in the seat facing his desk, teacup in hand, waiting.

He remained standing, behind the desk with the light shining in through the window.

"Very well…"

*D*earest Elspeth and James
What a delight it was to hear you are married. We literally jumped for joy. We would have given anything to see you become man and wife but under the circumstances we know why you could not wait. We will look forward to having you visit Maidstone at your earliest convenience.

Lord Farraday's letter in regards to the wedding was very vivid. We felt we were there as he described the garden, Delia as bridesmaid, the wedding feast and so much more. Mr Thomas added he felt truly honoured to be there.

Louisa is in marvellous health. To see her body grow and change is a wonder to me. And I await the arrival of our child with both excitement and anticipation.

Now down to business. We continue the investigations. We have discovered Alexander has bought a small farm not far from your estate. He used another name, a Mr Brood. But the agent assures us it was Alexander Thompson. I tell you this so you can discover where it is and watch the place. If he still has plans for Elspeth, this may be important. Attached is the possible address and map location. I suggest a twenty-four-hour vigil.

He has gone to ground since the tragic episode at Skye. No one saw him leave and no one has seen him at his home in Aberdeen or his usual haunts. Also, we have no idea where George and Oliver are. Both fathers returned to their estates. They have been telling of Charles MacDonald disgracing them, but no one seems to believe their stories. Confirming to me these men are not well liked in your society either. I know they are not much liked here in London.

I will write more the moment I hear more.
Your friend
Chalanor

"Well, what a turn up. A farm nearby?" He continued to look at the letter.

"What are your thoughts, my dear? Can we have someone check this farm out? I mean see if there are any signs of him being there?"

"I can certainly arrange to have it happen."

"I think it confirms for me he has no intention of giving up. I think he will try to get me, sooner rather than later."

"Over my dead body."

"I do not want you dead. Nor do I want him to catch me. We need to outsmart him. We have to come up with a way I am never alone, at least outside these walls."

"I am glad you are calm about this, my dear."

"Being upset will not help me. We must corner him, safely and not allow him to corner me. Now my dear, can we continue on the next letter?"

James sat in the chair behind his desk.

He cleared his throat.

"*My dear Elspeth and James,*
Oh, how good that sounds.

We continue the investigations. There are many things concerning us, and the Lords are checking even the smallest details. They have rounded up ten men of the ton, who are said to be a member of what we are now calling the FA Club. Four are denying any membership. The other six are being very useful and giving much detail to the events they have witnessed or been a part of. They have been placed in a secure part of prison and have no privileges. But they hope to be treated well in the long term, as they tell us all they know.

Two of the six admit to being involved in actual killings and branding. All in the past six months since Alexander has been in charge. Only one of the ten is believed to be part of the original group.

We have surmised that Alexander has spent the last year recruiting new members. It would seem there was not more than five members when Freddie was alive and were much more discreet than the gentlemen who have since joined the group. This is still too many but gives us hope we can find all of the men involved.

I have attached a list of the ten men in our prison.

(James held up a separate piece of paper.)

I have also attached a list of suspects in the Scottish society who may also be a part of the club, as per the information received from the six who are cooperating.

(He held up another sheet of paper.)

We have confirmed the farm is Hilltop Farm on your northern boundary. I will write again soon.

Your friend

Chalanor

"Do you know any of the names on the lists?"

"Yes, but they do not surprise me. All except one, Hugh Burbidge. He is a good friend of Lucas. Not the sort of young man I believe would take part in this sort of thing."

"That is interesting. Lucas and I are having a chat this afternoon. Perhaps he has become aware of his involvement and plans to tell us."

"But why is he not telling me?"

"I think he is embarrassed my dear, and wants to tell me so I can tell you. The gentle touch of a woman? Do not fret. I will come to you and reveal what he said as soon as we have had our conversation."

James looked at his calm and wonderful wife, glad to know she was coping with all this. He picked up the third letter.

"Dear friend,

A brief note to let you know I am on my way by carriage to Perth. From there I will rent a horse to ride to your estate. News of a concerning nature has reached us and I wish to tell you in person rather than by letter. I should arrive at your estate on the Thursday afternoon in the last week of September.

Will see you then.

Chalanor

. . .

"**W**hat on earth could it be?"

"It must be of great import if he is leaving Louisa to come to us directly. Now I am worried." She was wringing her hands and colour had reached her cheeks.

He got up from his chair and came to her, taking her in his embrace.

"Let us not fret. He will be here tomorrow afternoon and then we will know. Now, let us have luncheon. Do I need to speak to Lucas?"

"No, my dear. Just let me chat to him and then I can let you know the issue. I do not want to have him despair. I will encourage him to speak with you. I also feel honoured he wishes to speak privately to me. Trust me."

"I do very easily, my love. I will leave the issue in your safe hands."

21

TELL THE TRUTH AND BE DAMNED

*L*ucas was quiet during luncheon. She watched him carefully and he was very distracted. She took James' hand every now and then and gave it a squeeze. She could tell he wanted to say something, but he also did not want to embarrass the boy. If he wanted to speak with her in private, she wanted him to trust she would do so and not tell his brother everything. Once she could find out what was wrong, she was sure she could get him to talk to James and keep nothing from him.

At the appointed time she walked to the stable. Lucas was waiting for her.

He bowed. She came over and gave him a hug.

"What is bothering you? I can tell you are not yourself."

"Elspeth, you know I love you like I would if I had a sister?"

"Of course. And you now have a sister. Me"

"I have been very foolish, and I am not sure where to start."

"At the beginning. When did you feel things started to go wrong?"

He smiled at her.

"Very well." He escorted her to some bales of hay and suggested she sit down. He sat next to her.

"When mother died, I was devastated. We spent a lot of time together. Even when she was sick."

She took his hand. "I remember when my mother and father died. I too was not myself. I do understand."

"I knew you would. I felt lost. I really did not have anyone to talk to. James was sad and helping father with his great loss. And for him well…"

"He lost the love of his life. Am I right?"

"Yes. I found it hard to think or to feel. I went to Edinburgh for a time and lost myself to the society and with young men my own age. I got into a situation I could not get out of. I realise now how stupid I was being."

He looked into her eyes. "Elspeth, I joined the club. Alexander's club."

"Oh Lucas. No. Please tell me you did not?"

"I went to the first meeting and they were all talking about the death of your brother. They were angry he had killed himself. They were calling him a coward. I was confused and did not understand why they were so angry. Alexander wanted me to join. But I did not understand what they did. If I had I would never have joined. But all my friends were interested in joining so I agreed. The next meeting was held at his home near Aberdeen."

"Lucas, tell me you didn't go."

"I did but I did not stay long. When I realised what they were about to do I started to leave. Even my best friend Hugh wanted to go. Alexander said we had to stay. Because we knew too much. If I left, he would have to kill me. I begged him to let us go. I said I would keep his secret and those of George and Oliver. He told me he would on one condition."

"Oh, dear God no, Lucas. No. You cannot hand me over to him."

"I will tell you the truth. I said I would let him know when you arrived in Skye but nothing more. He agreed but said if anything happened to him, he would be sure I was implicated. I would be accused of murder, not him. Since then, I have done everything I could to keep him away from you. I even told him as late as I could about Skye, so he had to get Oliver and George to bring him along instead of waiting to be invited. He was very angry with me."

"Lucas. I believe you. Alexander can twist things around. I know what he is capable of doing. But you need to tell your brother. We need to make sure we can protect you too."

"But he tried to kill my brother. I was sure he would then try to kill me. I thought once we were home, we could escape him. But…"

"But what, Lucas. Tell me."

He placed his hand inside his coat pocket and drew out a missive. He handed it to her. She opened it and read it out loud.

*Y*ou will bring her to me, or I will kill all of you. And do not think that I cannot. I can and I will. *Top of Mount Dunsinane, Saturday at 3pm. If you do not, I will start picking you off one by one. You will all die.*

A.

*L*ucas. That is three days from now."

"I am not taking you to him. I would die first."

"I believe you, but this might be our chance to catch him. And put a stop to this. Please come with me to James and you can tell him what you told me."

"But he and you could have been killed and they killed Morag. I am a part of this whether I want to be or not."

"You have been blackmailed. Did you know he was going to kill Morag?"

"No. Her murder came as a complete shock. I didn't even know he was bedding her."

"I know you have been forced to do this. We can fix this. Please let us go to James and tell him."

"I will but please stay with me. If you are with me, I know we are both safe. I do not trust Alexander. This is all my fault."

She leaned over to hug him, and he hugged her back.

"Please forgive me?"

She stood and took his hand.

"I will stay with you. And you are forgiven."

───────

$\mathcal{H}$e was holding on to his temper. A red-hot flash of heat went through him. His face was hot and getting hotter by the minute.

"Oh, damn! Oh, damn! Why? Why?"

He wanted to yell and scream and hit something. Elspeth's eyes were pleading with him to stay calm. He waited till his brother finished his confession before he said a word. Lucas kept his head down and waited. He had been stupid. Stupid beyond anything he could imagine his brother ever doing.

"This feels like a betrayal."

"Yes James. One I hate myself for."

"What on earth were you thinking?"

Lucas did not respond. How could he?

"What you have done has placed us all in danger."

"Yes James. I am heartbroken. I had no idea what I was getting involved in. Please forgive me."

He stood from his chair behind his desk and came around to stand before his brother.

"I want your promise, on your life, you will do all you can to protect my wife."

"I will swear any oath, to do so. I love my new sister and will never hurt her or allow anyone else to hurt her. I will protect her with my life."

He took his brother by the hand and into his embrace. "I am sorry I did not help you with your grief."

"You were helping our father. I am sorry I behaved like a child. Forgive me."

"You are my brother. There is nothing to forgive. Thank you for telling me now and not after Alexander had acted."

"I would die before I let his hand touch Elspeth."

"Well said, brother. Well said."

"Now, we need to decide what to do. But we should wait till Chalanor arrives." He looked at his wife who then responded.

"Yes. If Chalanor has more information, then we need to know."

"I did not know he was coming." said Lucas.

James picked up the missive from his desk and handed it to his brother.

Lucas read it. "I wonder. Perhaps he has heard of my connection and wishes to break the news to you in person rather than by letter."

"Perhaps. We will find out tomorrow."

---

*I*t was late but near her beloved James, she could not sleep or think straight. His touch made her dream of what he could do, and a smile crossed her face. She gave a little shiver. Too much had been going on. She was happy Lucas had revealed his secret but disturbed at just how close Alexander could get to her. This man was relentless. But she knew that Lucas would defend her. James drew her into his embrace.

"Do you think that anyone else in the house could betray us?"

He kissed her head.

"I don't think so. After all Lucas did not succumb when he realised what they were up to. He was merely looking for a way to get out of a situation he did not want to be in. Our staff are good people. I don't think they could fall for Alexander's twisted words."

"Even the maids? So many have fallen under his spell."

"Yes, even they. Walker has warned them of his tricks and lies. He has told them at my request. They have been given a description of what he looks like and what he can do.

"I hope you are right."

"I will not let you out of my sight."

"You might not get the choice."

"Then others will be near you. The staff are aware of the situation and you have become dear to them already. Just ask Mrs K. We will make sure all is well."

"But I worry now about Lucas. What if Alexander tries to kill him because he won't do what he says?"

"Dearest. We will sort this out. I have some ideas and once Chalanor arrives we will make a plan."

She held him closer as he again kissed the top of her head. She wanted to believe he was right. But squiggles of doubt and concern rose in her stomach. And it did not feel comfortable. She was unwell from the concern that kept building around her. This is not part of the life that she had dreamed of.

He wanted to do all he could to take her mind off the whole mess Alexander had created. He made slow, romantic love to her. Giving her pleasure as he knew no one else could and she devoured it. Her hunger for him was strong. He could feel every muscle and sinew pull him closer to her. She could not get enough. And neither could he. Life with Elspeth was all he ever wanted. He could not imagine her not being here enjoying what he did to her. He loved her beyond reason. Beyond fate. Beyond life itself.

He would do all he could to save his beautiful wife from the mad man out there. He knew his staff would do the same. He also knew his brother would not betray her. With Chalanor arriving tomorrow, they would set a trap to catch a mad man. They had to win. There was no alternative he was prepared to accept.

22

JOY OR PAIN?

Breakfast was at eight-thirty as usual. Their usual. She loved the routine they had established since they arrived at Collace House. James was doing all he could to make her comfortable. Like today. This morning a group of dress fitters from The House of Glenmore in Edinburgh were coming to measure and help her create a new wardrobe of clothing. A trousseau, a wedding gift from her husband. He wanted her to have fashionable attire for when they would be making appearances both in the neighbourhood and in Perth. And eventually in Edinburgh. Especially as the weather was getting colder, something she still had to get used to. She needed more warm clothing.

Right on nine, they arrived and were ushered into the dayroom by Walker. He came to fetch her.

"I have placed them in the day room ma'am, and they await your arrival."

"Thank you, Walker. Delia, will you join me? I could do with your knowledge of Scottish society and weather."

"I would be happy to help. Walker, could we have pen and paper so I can take notes, to be sure we miss nothing."

"Wonderful idea. James, you will let me know when Chalanor arrives."

"Oh yes please. I am so excited he is coming. Not why he is coming but it will be wonderful to see him. I have not seen him in such a long time."

Elspeth watched the excitement as Delia shared her joy. She too looked forward to Chalanor's arrival. From the first, Elspeth had told her everything that was going on. Delia herself has been such a support. Though all were concerned as to what Alexander was up to. A small smile lifted her lips. Delia looked happy.

"I assure you my dear, Walker or Jasper will be the first to tell you." He nodded at Walker who nodded back to his master.

"Now go and create a wonderful assortment of clothing. I want you to look wonderful in everything you create. Remember money is no object. You are to have the best." He stood and came to her and kissed her playfully on her nose.

"Thank you, my dear. I will do as I am instructed."

James headed for his study and she and Delia made a beeline for the day room.

"I am sure, my lady, you have chosen all you need. Shall we check Miss Delia's list?" Added Madam Kathrine, chief seamstress of the House of Glenmore.

Delia read out the list and she mentally took stock. Everything except for one thing, was on the list.

"Delia, can you go to the kitchen and arrange for morning tea for us all."

Delia smiled and blushed and left the room.

"Madam Kathrine, can we arrange three-or four-night garments of a different nature, than comfortable?"

"Of course, my dear. Have a look at these drawings. As a new bride, I am sure these will be what you desire."

They were beautiful. Lace and see through. Provocative but special. Flattering and sensual. Just for her and James. This would be a wonderful gift for him as well as her.

"Yes madam. I will have one of each of these four designs. They will be perfect."

"I will add them to the list."

Delia re-entered the room. "Tea will arrive in five minutes, Elspeth. Let us sit down. Madam, will you join us?"

The poor woman was surprised. "Thank you but I must head back to Edinburgh today. I want to get a start on your order as quickly as I can. I will send a missive, madam, when you can expect the order to be complete."

"Very well Madam Kathrine. Thank you for coming to me. It is very much appreciated."

"You are most welcome, madam. I will gather my things and take my leave."

She and her two assistants gathered the notes, tape measures and material swatches and left the room.

Elspeth sat down and Delia came over to the chaise and sat next to her.

"That was a good morning's work. You will have beautiful outfits and accessories. James will not be disappointed."

"I hope not. It is a lot of money."

"Yes, but he can afford it. He wants what is best for you. I envy you."

"Oh Delia, I am sorry. I should have let you pick something out."

"No. You mistake my meaning. I envy you. The wonderful relationship you have with James."

"You will still not reveal your person of interest?"

"No. Not yet. I have both time and thinking to do. I need to work out what is right for me. I can already see what is right for you."

"I never thought that I would marry. But I never realised how much I loved James until I saw him again. Then you could say all of a sudden, the pieces of the jigsaw, pieces of my life, fell into place. I need James."

"Which is very good to know. Because even a blind man can see James needs you. You are meant for each other."

Tea was brought in and they sat chatting and sipping the beautiful brown liquid.

"Can I intrude on this pleasant gathering?" It was James. He had a small chest under his arm.

"Naturally, my dear. Please come and sit by me." She winked at Delia who giggled and got up to sit in the chair opposite her.

"I am not intruding?" he asked with a grin on his lips.

"No, my dear. Having you nearby is wonderful." And she meant it. His grin grew.

"I should have given these to you earlier. Lucas and I were just discussing them."

He opened the small chest that was now sitting on his lap. She leaned over and looked inside.

"These are the family jewels. Some are of no value except sentimental. But each tells a story."

He reached in and picked out a broach. It had purple stones in the shape of a flower.

"This was my grandmother's. She always wore it. Mother did, but only on special occasions out of respect for her."

"It is beautiful."

"This one," he reached in and pulled out a string of pearls. "My father gave to my mother. They are Scottish pearls. Did you know that the Romans invaded Britain for the Scottish pearls? You will find none better." He placed the chest next to him, got up and went behind her and placed them around her neck.

"Pearls are better when they are warmed by the body. You must wear these."

"I will James." She ran them through her fingers. They were smooth and fine. What a luxury. She touched her other pearl, the one that belonged to her mother.

"I think that the two, look magnificent together." he added. James sat down again and placed the chest back in his lap. He started to look through it again.

She stood and went to the mirror. She looked at the lone pearl. And suddenly she could see it. It was not alone anymore. Just as she was no longer alone. Elspeth looked down at the strand of pearls. They shone and glistened with a pinkish tinge. She had a small strand that her parents had given her which she still owned. These were so much more glorious. In part because James had given them to her. And they were old. Part of the great family she was now part of. It was humbling and she was honoured. And he was right. The single pearl hanging there both looked good and felt right. It was a perfect match for the pearls James had just given her. She was content. Part of a family as her single pearl now belonged with the others. She came and sat down again next to James.

"Ah. This is what I was looking for." He pulled out a ring. Made of gold and it had a stone in it. Rich deep blue. A sapphire. The stone was square and on either side was a diamond, also square, but smaller.

"You have a beautiful gold band on your wedding finger. I would not have you change for the world. Will you do me the honour of wearing this on your other hand?"

She reached over and he took her hand and placed it on her finger. It fitted perfectly. As if it had been made specifically for her. She looked down at it. She could see into the very heart of the stone. It captured her imagination.

"I adore it, James. I truly do." The tears built up. She looked at the stone again as her sight blurred.

"Thank you from my heart."

Delia came over and kneeled in front of her and took her hand.

"It is beautiful. Magical. What is the story connected with this one?"

James smiled at Delia.

"It goes back two hundred years. It belonged to a great, great, great, aunt. Well, let us just say a great aunt. She fell in love with a Dutch trader who travelled to Dundee often to trade. He loved her also and eventually they married. He came to live in her land, so she still had her family nearby. After one trip he brought her back this ring. Telling her the deep blue stone was to remind her of his travels on the deep blue sea. But the diamonds would remind her he would always come back to her."

"How lovely."

"But there is more. He was shipwrecked. And after being late on his return, word came the ship had been lost with all hands. She would not believe it. She knew he was alive, and he would come back. For two years her family tried all they could to convince her he was not coming back. She would not believe it. Then one day he came walking up the road to the house where they lived. People were following him, cheering, and rejoicing. He was alive. His wife, hearing the ruckus, came out. She ran to her husband knowing it was him, even though he was bearded and scruffy."

Oh, what a tale. She became breathless and had tears in her eyes as he told it.

"He never did go back to sea but became a farmer and lived to a very old age with his beloved. I will take you to the local Parish churchyard and show you their grave. They had a wonderful life together. She kept her faith in him coming back to her. I want you to keep your faith, I will let nothing, or no one come in the way of our happiness."

She looked at James. She could feel every bit of truth in what he was saying. She looked down at Delia who was crying.

"I am so happy for you both. Believe in the truth of love. Please excuse me." She got up and left the room, still crying. Elspeth was sure it was from the story not from sadness. She would check on her later.

"Thank you, James. I will wear it in honour of your ancestors and also because you love me. And I too will believe in your promise." She leaned in and kissed him. A kiss that lengthened and lasted for some time.

They heard a cough.

"I dare say you get to do this quite often now. But may I interrupt?"

It was Chalanor. Delia was standing behind him with a huge smile on her face and holding his hand.

Elspeth jumped up and threw herself into her dear friend's arms.

"The day is now complete." She added. "We are here together. All of us."

23

TELLING THE TRUTH

The joy seemed to permeate through the house. Delia was happy, James was also, and she rejoiced in the reuniting of friends. They had luncheon with great joy because they were all together.

Chalanor had made better time than he had thought. He was not expected till the afternoon, but the early arrival was welcomed. They also did not waste time in getting to the heart of why Chalanor had come.

Chalanor looked at Lucas. "It is about you Lucas, in part."

"I have told Elspeth and James of my foolish mistake. I do not want to be connected to them."

"I knew you would tell them. I knew you would not get involved. But it is not only that. I knew they would try to blackmail you. They have done so to other fine fellows in London. My main concern was, George and Oliver have been detained in London. They thought society there would know nothing of the antics or involvement with Alexander. They were wrong."

"Are they restrained?" She asked. Her heart was beating faster than she was comfortable with. These days were taking a toll on her wellbeing. She felt lightheaded and sickly.

"Yes. They were immediately taken to the magistrates. The lords presented what evidence they had already obtained showing the links between George and Oliver with Alexander and Freddie. They have been arrested. Oliver has kept his mouth shut and will say nothing. George however has been squealing like a pig. He has been giving names, places etc."

"What wonderful news. They are believing him, are they not?"

"Undoubtedly," continued Chalanor. "However, what we discovered, places more danger on all of you here. So, I was determined to come and let you know. Perhaps something can be done. You see, Alexander has promised to kill Lucas as well as Elspeth. He has every intention to hunt you both down. It came straight from George's rantings."

"This is disconcerting, but I have known that the mad man would hunt me down. It was my foolish error putting us in danger. I do not care about me, but I do care what happens to Elspeth."

"But I care about you. You are James' brother; my brother and I am sick of this mess my own flesh and blood has created. Freddie was not the man I thought I knew." She stood and walked to the window. Her concern was greater than it had ever been. "This has to stop." Her head was pounding, as was her heart.

"I agree. But you need not be hunted down. You were his sister not his accomplice. Besides, it is Alexander who has the unnatural streak in his nature not you. And he has made the club bigger than even your brother had intended." Chalanor concluded.

James threw his napkin on the table. "What can we do? He has not been sighted in the area. If he knows what has become of Oliver and George, then we know he will not follow them to London. He will bide his time and then come and fulfil his promise against my brother and my wife." He got up and placed his arms around her.

"That is true. But George assured us he is here in this area. So, we may have to take even a small piece of information and discover him before he reveals himself. We have the advantage over him. He thinks he is well hidden." Chalanor folded his napkin and placed it on the table. He got up and went to stand next to Elspeth and James and took her hand. "You have been and will be a dear friend to myself and Louisa. We need to do something to both protect you and to bring this mad man to justice."

She lowered her head. This was getting out of hand and she knew it. Too many people were involved, and someone was bound to get hurt. She loved her new home. But this was a place of peace for her and she wanted to keep it so. How could she live here if she were constantly looking over her shoulder?

"What of the threat to Lucas?" She turned and looked at the men around her.

"Alexander wants me. Lucas, he thinks, will be the go between. So why not pursue that line?"

"You mean the meeting on the mount this Saturday?" Lucas added. "Elspeth, we cannot. It places you in too much danger."

"My dear, Lucas is correct. We cannot use you as bait no matter how much he wants you."

"But if we know more than he thinks then perhaps we can. After all it is up to us to outsmart him."

"But my dearest, if something goes wrong, I could lose you. I will not hear of it."

"What are you talking about?" Chalanor pleaded.

They explained the missive Lucas had received.

"This does put us on the front foot. We know more than he. So, Elspeth is right. We could outsmart him and catch him once and for all."

"Not if it puts her in harm's way."

"But I have to. I don't want anyone else getting hurt because of me."

"My love, it is not you. People make their own choices, and you cannot be held accountable for their mistakes."

"But I can bring this to an end and stop it from going any further."

The silence was clear. She was right and they could now see it. Although her head still drummed, she was revived. Her idea just might work.

———

She was laying on the bed with her eyes closed. He silently closed the bedroom door and came and sat on the bed next to her. He watched her chest rise slowly then deflate. She was asleep. He could see she was unwell. He could also see she was determined to get Alexander caught and out of her life for good.

She stirred.

"Are you not concerned that the staff may talk?"

"Let them talk. I am with my wife and don't care what they think."

"What is wrong James?"

"You. Your determination to be bait for Alexander's capture."

"No one else can be bait. It is me he wants."

"I don't want you in danger."

"I know. But I will be in danger until he is caught. Come lay down with me."

James laid down next to her and took her in his arms.

"You are not well."

"It is but a headache. I am sure it will not last long."

He held her closer. "I don't want you to do this."

"I know. But who else can? You have all the manpower and ability to keep me safe. He won't succeed in having me."

"But there is a possibility he might kill you before we can reach you."

"Yes, but with all the plans in place I don't think it can happen. Lucas will be with me. We know he will do all he can to protect me."

"There are no guarantees."

"No, but I do not want to live my life waiting and wondering when he will strike. We have found each other again and I want to live my life with you and all of what it will give us. So, you will just have to save me."

"Very well but I will never be far from you. Do you hear me?"

"Yes, my James. I hear you and I expect you to be very close. Now let us rest."

He closed his eyes. Soon he could feel her gentle breathing and knew that she was again asleep. He did not like the arrangements. But he bowed to her decision. She would not live a life worth living while Alexander was on the scene. He had to help her rid him from her life. Once and for all.

***

*L*ucas went to the ruined wall.

"The stage is set. She will come. She has no idea you are here. She thinks you have gone to London to be with George and Oliver."

"Good. You have played your part. I will see you on Saturday at three."

"I will be here. With her."

"At last. My lust for her will be fulfilled."

Lucas headed back home. He hated putting his sister in danger. But he would protect her. His brother would catch this bastard and end his reign of terror.

24

BEAUTIFUL DAYS

When she woke on Friday morning, she still had a headache, but it was not as bad as the day before. She would have been happy to stay in bed. But she knew if she did, James would never let her go up the mount tomorrow.

Jasper brought in their tea and she and James enjoyed it in front of the window in their room.

"I plan to spend the day with you today, Els."

"Oh, how lovely. What shall we do?"

"It is cool but if we wear our coats, I thought we could ride around the estate and you can meet some of our tenants."

"I would love to. But no guards or servants with us please. Just the two of us. And not on horses. In a curricle?"

"As you wish, my lady. Your wish is my command."

"Well, that gives me great power. And can we visit the village?"

"Of course. It will be a pleasant drive. We can stop at the inn and have luncheon."

"Wonderful."

*A*fter breakfast they strolled around to the stables. A curricle was waiting for them. This was not a town curricle but a sturdy country one. The pair of horses were beautiful blacks. Although she did not like to ride, she loved the look of horses and could understand why so many people loved the majestic animals. In a curricle she was as close to a horse as she wanted to be.

He helped her up into the seat and then went around to the other side and got into the machine himself.

Soon they were riding out the main drive and heading towards the village. She knew they would head to the village first as she wanted to see it. Mainly because she wanted to know the sorts of things she could get from there. She had told James this morning it is what she wanted to do first. The breeze rushed by her hatted head. It was refreshing and soon there were no mores signs of a headache. And she felt better than she had in days.

"The time is flying by since we were married. We have had so many rich experiences, have we not?"

"We have, my dear. The most important being the love we share with each other."

"Very true James. And I love making love with you."

"I certainly hope so." He laughed. It was a laugh of joy. He was happy and so was she.

Alexander came to her thoughts again and she hated the idea. She wanted to be happy with no thoughts of evil intentions or grubby plans. She wanted only to be at peace in her new life with James. Shaking her head to get rid of the thoughts, she looked at James.

"Is this the side of the village the dowager house is on? Perhaps we can drop in and see your father?"

"We can. We are only a few minutes away from the house."

"It seems strange he is not in the big house. But I understand why he wants to live here. I hope he adjusts to the changes. He has been such a support to us both before and now we are married."

They continued to talk about experiences and future plans until at last James pulled up in front of the dowager house.

A stable hand came running from the rear of the house to take the reins. James lifted her from the curricle and placed her down in front of him. He took her in his arms as the horses were led away and he kissed her.

"There are definite advantages to being married to you, James. Your kisses are one of them." She laughed out loud and he joined in.

They went to the front door and knocked. An elderly butler answered the door.

"Master James. Welcome. This must be your lovely wife, sir?"

"It is McMaster. Meet Mistress Elspeth."

"How do you do McMaster?"

"I cannot complain, madam." He looked at James. "Your father sir, is in the breakfast room." He turned and escorted them to the left of the hall. He opened the door.

"Master James and his wife Elspeth, sir."

Raeburn stood as they entered the room.

"How delightful to see you." and took his daughter in law into a hug. "Please sit down and give me your first impressions of the estate. McMaster, tea for my guests."

"Yes sir." And he turned and left the room, closing the door behind him.

"It is good to see you Raeburn. Have you recovered from our trip from Skye?"

"I have, my dear. I feel at peace with the world knowing you are in the big house with my son."

She could feel the heat rise into her cheeks.

"Thank you, Raeburn. It is a pleasure to be at home in the big house."

"Now, tell me what you have been doing."

For the next hour she shared her ideas and her love of the staff at the house. Raeburn smiled at her constantly. He seemed genuinely happy both with her answers and her excitement. This made her feel even more at home.

James also shared the more recent news about the 'club' and their concerns.

"She has to be kept safe. If Alexander should harm her…?" She watched her father-in-law grow red-faced.

"With what we have in place, I believe Elspeth will be safe but seconds away from someone of the estate or one of us. I will do all I can to protect my wife. I don't like this arrangement, but I believe she will be safe."

"I certainly hope you are correct, and he has no idea his partners in crime have been captured and detained?"

"We believe he is yet to hear that news."

"I will keep you informed, Father."

"I will be at the big house at three o'clock in the afternoon. And you, my dear, need to promise me that you will not take any risks to your person."

"I promise, Raeburn. I just want this to stop."

"I understand, my dear."

———

Taking their leave, they were soon on their way. Elspeth was still bright and happy. She was relaxed to have seen Raeburn and know all was well with him. She had become concerned for him ever since she found out his mother had died. Watching her interact with his father warmed him and reminded him of the reasons he had always loved her. Her kindness, concern for others and love of people in general.

They continued to the village. The drive was pleasant. The leaves on the trees were bronzing and reddening. Many of the leaves were flicking up in the breeze the curricle created. He found comfort in the rustling of the leaves as they drove on.

He pointed out the small haberdashery and the farming shop. The blacksmith and the inn. There was a shoemaker and a weaver's hall where much weaving in the district was done. A small shop front displayed general clothing you could have mended or bought from a Mrs Grimley. The buildings were nearly all made of sandstone and added to the tranquil feel the village gave.

He parked his curricle at the inn and he and Elspeth walked around the street of the village. He introduced her to many of the inhabitants and store clerks. He had a great deal of pleasure watching them bow and smile at his Els. She was well accepted by all.

Many welcomed her and gave small samples of their wares or showed them through their shops. Her smile never left her face. They stopped at a shop front that simply said, Estate. He entered and held the door open for Elspeth.

"Estate. What does this shop do?"

"It is maintained by us. We have an agent here, Mr David Dunstan."

He turned as Mr Dunstan came towards him.

"May I introduce you to my wife Mr Dunstan."

A man of similar age to them came towards her. He bowed and she curtsied.

"It is a pleasure to meet you, madam. I have heard wonderful things about you."

"Really? From whom? I barely know anyone here."

"From Mrs K, madam. She is my mother-in-law."

"Oh, how delightful. I had no idea Mrs K had children, and so close by."

"My Myra is cook to Master Raeburn at the dowager house. Which is where I am his secretary as well. You will find me there in the afternoons."

"Now I am intrigued. What then do you do here?"

"We are a small village and as you are aware, many villages are disappearing due to many Scots immigrating to America and such places. In the mornings I am here and match up any of the villagers with jobs that can be done on the estate."

"How wonderful."

"We have jobs for short periods and permanent ones. Villagers and those from the estate needing work, come to see me here in the village and we do what we can. Then I go back to the dowager house and help his lordship with his correspondence. This may include meeting with your husband on estate matters."

"This is a wonderful idea and very long term in thinking."

"It was an idea your husband had and was gladly accepted by his lordship. It has helped us to keep many of the estate families here in the village and on many of the estate farms. We even have families from other estates requesting to join us."

"I am truly impressed."

James took her hand and faced her.

"You should know many of the men are keeping us safe at present. They are watching and waiting, for any unusual activities or people in the neighbourhood. It is all coordinated from here."

She turned and looked at Mr Dunstan. "Thank you, sir. I am deeply grateful for all this effort."

"Our pleasure, madam. We protect our own."

He watched her face grow red. She smiled gently.

"Please sir, show me around."

And she and Mr Dunstan looked around the rooms which stored equipment and held paperwork as was needed. He followed her movements as she again slipped into mistress of the manor. He never doubted that she was right for the position, let alone for him.

*A*s they walked into the inn, he could see Els was deep in thought. The inn keeper escorted them to a private room on the ground floor. It was warm and very cosy. The room was lightly painted and had some delicate and beautiful paintings on the wall.

"This room is very homely. I like it."

"This is the estate's private room. It is used by the family and guests when it is needed. The paintings were done by my mother. I would dearly like you to place some of your own here, one day."

She wandered around the room looking at each painting in turn. The first was clearly a view from the main bedroom window out to the Firth of Tay. It was one of his favourites. It was clear and crisp and clearly showed the view as it is. Els stood in front of it for some time.

The second picture was a painting of the stables at the big house. It even had two horses in it. He liked this one as well. His mother loved horses to paint but would never go near them to ride. She had a fall as a young woman and never rode again. He knew that Els had a bad fall just over a year ago. She still liked horses but did not want to ride them. The similarity had not escaped him.

She wandered to the third picture. Here she stayed for some time. The inn keeper came in and he ordered their luncheon while she stayed captivated with the scene. He sat and watched her, waiting to hear her response.

"This one is so beautiful. The big house in the foreground and the dowager house in the distance. I know you cannot see this view from the house. Where did your mother paint this one?"

She turned towards him awaiting his response.

"Up on top of Mount Dunsinane."

"Ahh. Yes, that would explain the perspective. This is breathtaking. I love this one."

"I am sure mother would appreciate your praise. I will take you up there and show you from where she painted it."

"I would like to see it from there."

She looked deeply into his eyes. He loved this woman with every inch of his being. One look and she told him wordlessly she loved him. She came over and sat down at the table opposite him. She was thoughtful again.

"We will get through this, my dearest." He took her hand. "I will let no one hurt you as long as I am alive."

"I know that James, with all my heart I know. But…"

"No buts Els…please."

"So long as he does not come after you, I know I am safe."

25

OH, WHAT A NIGHT

The drive back to the big house was wonderful. The breeze was fresh, and the leaves still blew around the wheels of the curricle. The sun poked through the clouds now and then to warm them with its rays. She and James talked about the beautiful luncheon of cold meats, warm bread, cheeses, and dried fruits they had at the inn. They spoke of the other paintings in the room, which consisted of eight all together. Each one a unique view of the house or a different part of the estate. They had chatted to many in the village and workers from the estate. Though they had spent the whole morning and lunchtime in the village and were yet to venture to the actual farms.

They pulled up to the house and Chalanor, Delia and Lucas were standing on the stairs, looking out towards the drive.

"I hope we have not kept you waiting?" James called as he descended the curricle. A stable hand appeared from the lower house and held the curricle as he again lifted his lovely wife down to the ground.

"Waiting? Why are they waiting?"

"We have worked out our plans for tomorrow afternoon and I

want you to know all of them so as to ease your mind. I know you have been fretting over it."

"Very well. Though I would not call it fretting. It is very much fear that consumes me. Fear of the man and what he can do."

"And we cannot have that." Chalanor said as he came down the steps. "Fear will hurt you whether he is near you or not."

"We need to get this right, my love."

"Where do you wish to go?"

"Let us go and sit under the tree."

"I will go and freshen up and come and join you in ten minutes." She turned and headed up the steps.

---

*D*elia was about to follow her, but he took her arm. "No, stay here. She needs a few moments to herself. I am concerned. We have had a lovely day, but she has been getting quieter as the day has progressed."

"That is understandable, James. Tomorrow must be of great concern to her. She fears not only for her own life but for the lives of those she loves."

"I agree. I wanted her to know where the people will be who will protect her. She will know there will be eyes on her at all times. Then perhaps she will see we will prevail, and she will be safe."

They all turned and went to the oak tree to the right of the big house. Under its branches were garden chairs and a table. The servants had cleaned them and placed afternoon tea there for them. The last of the items were being placed as they came to the table. The rustling of the leaves again gave him comfort. He could not explain it. They just did.

They sat in the chairs. Lucas was making his way to them over the lawn.

"I fear for Lucas, too. This mad man wants them both." Added Chalanor.

"But we can protect them both, can't we?" asked Delia.

"I do hope so, but who knows what he plans to do? We can only do what we can and help them both as needs arise. We must think like him so we can be prepared."

Delia shivered. "I don't like the thought. Who would ever want to think like him?"

"I agree but think his way we must."

In her dressing room she got out of her morning dress and slipped into another. She added a shawl. She left the clothing on the chair and was about to leave when Lottie entered.

"Is there anything I can do for you, madam?"

"Yes, thank you Lottie. I have changed. Can you arrange for the items on the chair to be cleaned please?"

"Certainly, madam." As Lottie went past her, she noticed a slight smell of whisky but shook it off. Her senses were heightened, and she could explain why. Lottie had probably cleaned up dishes in the kitchen.

As she went down the stairs at the front of the house, she paused and grabbed the railing next to her. She looked towards the group under the oak tree. They were blurred in her sight. She felt the hand of someone reach around her waist.

"Please excuse me, ma'am. But I saw you and you seemed unsteady on your feet. Can I help?"

"Yes Walker. Please help me to sit on the step."

He helped her down then sat next to her.

He snapped his fingers and said, "Water," and she heard footsteps running from where she sat.

Her head was spinning. "I don't know what is wrong. I have been feeling lightheaded for days."

Walker handed her a glass of water and as he did, she looked up into the eyes of her beloved James.

She took a sip and then everything went black.

———

"Mrs K, you cannot be sure. We have only been married about three weeks. How could she have fallen with child so soon?"

"Sir, there is many a woman who has fallen from the first time. I for one would feel ill almost immediately. Besides what other explanation could there be?"

She heard the words but still felt distant from where the words were spoken. They seemed far away, like in another room. She tried to move and could not. She stopped trying and continued to listen to the conversation spinning around her. She tried to focus in on a voice. Of her James.

"Then under no circumstances is she going up the mount tomorrow."

She lifted her hand and James took hold of it.

"Els, are you alright?"

"Yes," and she slowly pulled herself into a sitting position. She was in the dayroom surrounded by almost everybody. Chalanor, Delia, Lucas, Mrs K, Walker, Lottie and a number of other maids and footmen.

"Really, I am alright."

"You fainted. If Walker had not noticed that you seemed unsure on your feet you may have fallen down the stairs." Concern was plastered all over his face. The smell of whisky was in the air again. Now she was smelling strange smells at ridiculous times.

"I am sure it is purely the stress of the past weeks which has unbalanced me. A good night's sleep and I will be fine."

"But what if you are with child?"

"I am sure it is only the stresses I have been under. Travelling, packing, getting married, late nights, new situations. Besides, we have only been married three weeks. I could not yet be with child. I think it is wishful thinking on everyone's part."

"When you are feeling better, we will go to the library and have our meeting. Then we will decide what is to be done."

"James, I am fine. Come Delia, help me get up and we will go to the library now."

Delia helped her to stand. She took a deep breath to steady herself. She hoped she gave the appearance of being her normal self.

They all made their way to the library. James escorted her to the chaise, and she sat down. "James I am fine. Truly."

"I will broker no excuse. Please put your feet up."

She did so. He did not seem to be convinced but he and Chalanor started the discussion anyway.

"Very well. Lucas and you will walk up the mount to the castle ruin. There is a clump of bushes next to the ruin and we will have a man there ready to act if need be."

She nodded.

"We believe he will take you down the north side of the mount to get to his newly acquired farm. We will place armed men closely together on that side to be sure you are always covered."

"What if he decides to take me down the mount another way to put you off the scent?" She asked carefully.

Chalanor responded this time.

"Each path off the mount will have a guard posted. If he tries to confuse us, we should find him very quickly."

"Meanwhile," James continued. "A group of us will go to the farmhouse and remove any other men who may be there. They will be sent straight to Perth. We will then position ourselves around the house so we can catch him unaware when he returns."

"It sounds like a good plan. I am sure all will be fine. Now let me have an early night and a long sleep in and I will be ready for three o'clock."

"My dear, I let you do this, but I feel you should not."

"I understand James, but if I do not do this, I am not sure the terror of this man will ever leave me. All will be well. Trust me."

———

*A*s they lay in bed together, he pondered her possible condition. Could she be expecting a child? Was it possible so soon? She was fast asleep, and he had no desire to waken her. But he could not shut his own mind down. All the possibilities ran through his brain.

He gently eased himself out of bed and went to the window to do his thinking. Could she be with child? What a blessing that would be. He saw the lights on at the dowager house but thought no more about it. Still, he wondered if the child was a boy or a girl. He pictured himself with a daughter running around the lawns. But she might not be. It seemed he was getting nowhere, so he grabbed his dressing gown and headed downstairs. As he made his way to his study, he thought of all the events of the last month. The wedding, different but what he had wanted for so long. Elspeth, in his arms and all the pleasure that had given them. Alexander trying to hurt her. Hurting him. But he could not shake the thought of Alexander. He wanted this mad man out of their lives, but it seemed a hopeless task, trying to get rid of him.

He poured himself a whisky and sat at his desk. What could he do to prevent Els going up the mountain? He turned and watched Chalanor and Lucas entering his study.

"You my friend cannot sleep either." Chalanor chortled.

"No. It evades me. And I see you two have escaped sleep as well."

"Too much is going on inside my head to allow sleep to settle." added Lucas.

"We are men of action and waiting does not help us. We want to see this done and over."

"True. And it would seem that father is the same." James said as he gazed into the dark night.

"What makes you say that?"

"I can just see lights on at the dowager house. When I looked out my bedroom window, I noted the house was lit up."

Lucas came to the window and looked towards the drive that led to the dowager house. "I had no idea this window offered a clear view to the house."

"James, why not dress and walk to father's and discuss the situation with him. Maybe then we can all get some sleep."

"Lucas, what a wonderful idea. He might have a way or a suggestion as to me keeping Elspeth from going up the mount."

"Why not ride?"

"It is but a mile and the less noise we make the less likely we are at waking the household. I for one would like Elspeth to continue sleeping."

"Then can I suggest that we dress and make our way to the gate. We can meet there and make our way to your father's."

"Yes. Let us go. I will see you both in ten minutes."

They all made their way back to their rooms.

He looked in on Els and could see she was still in a deep sleep.

He went to his dressing room and dressed. He took his heavy coat as well and went out the back way from the house and walked towards the main gate. There was an unease in him he could not explain. He had slipped a small pistol in the pocket of his coat. Just in case.

26

SURPRISE

Chalanor was waiting as he reached the gate. In a few moments Lucas arrived. They walked in silence for a while. But he could keep quiet no longer.

"I am concerned."

"We all are." said Chalanor

"No, you misunderstand me. I am concerned because father's lights are on at the dowager house. I have been thinking more on it."

"Why?" Lucas added.

"Father is an early to bed man. This is out of character."

"Perhaps he is restless as we are, about Elspeth and what Alexander plans to do."

"He could be but, it just feels wrong."

"Well, if it concerns you, we will not make ourselves known when we get there and just have a look around."

James thought for a moment. "Yes. I may be overthinking things, but I do not trust Alexander. It is just like him to take his frustration out on someone else."

Lucas stopped walking. The other two gentlemen stopped and turned to look at him.

"What is it, brother?"

"Now you come to it, I remember a tale Alexander told. I will not bore you with it all, but something sticks in my throat every time I think of it. He said he would kill anyone to get the woman he wanted, even a lord if he had to."

"And you think he may aim to get father?"

"I haven't until now. But I would not put it past Alexander. He could boast to his so-called friends, he killed a lord if he did kill father. And when I reported to him, he seemed distant, distracted. He was unconcerned about my coming as if he already had plans to do what he wanted without my help. Besides, he did say he would pick us off one at a time."

"Normally, I would dismiss your concerns as wild imaginings, but Alexander is capable of confusing and changing his plans. I say we sneak into the house and see what could be afoot."

"I think we are in agreement."

"Let's keep going."

They continued their walk to the house but now there seemed to be an increase in the pace to get there.

***

"*L*ook, there are lights on both upstairs and down. This is not right. Something is amiss." James whispered.

"Then let us go around the back and quietly make our way through the house." Chalanor stepped forward and went to the side of the house. They listened but could hear no noise. They went slowly and quietly to the kitchen door. The kitchen was a large building separate from the house at the rear. No lights were on.

Lucas lifted his finger to indicate quiet and moved towards the door. He opened it but could hear nothing or see anything amiss in the moonlight. They moved slowly up the covered walkway to the back door of the house. It was ajar.

Each of them looked at each other. This was wrong. Perhaps it was wise they had been cautious. Again, Lucas lifted his finger to indicate quiet. He went through the door looked down and then came out again. He came closer to them and whispered. "McMaster is on the floor. He appears to be dead. I would say a gunshot as he is laying in a pool of blood."

"Then this would have been tonight. The cook would have been here all day. She has already left if the kitchen is in darkness and in order. Only my father and McMaster would have been in the house this evening. We have to hope father is alright and is being held captive by Alexander." James shook his head, stunned to think his feelings of something not being right had proved true. He had to trust his intuition more.

Chalanor whispered, "I suggest we carefully go through the house together listening as we go and see if your father is either dead or has been taken hostage."

"I would like to believe he is alive."

Chalanor nodded at him.

"We must rescue him if we can. Perhaps we can catch Alexander and this bad dream can come to an end." James looked at the others and they nodded to him.

"James, please allow me to lead." Lucas did not take his eyes from him. He in turn looked deeply into his brother's eyes and though no words were spoken he could hear his brother say. *'Let me do this, do this to redeem myself.'* James nodded. Lucas turned and entered the house. He followed and Chalanor came up behind him.

*T*hey slowly moved around the house. Each room they listened or looked through key holes to see what they could see. The ground floor was clear. They turned their attention to the first floor. "Beware the 7th and 10th step as they are prone to squeaking." James whispered.

"How on earth do you know that?" asked Lucas.

"Simple, I wanted them fixed but father would not hear of it. He said a squeak never hurt anyone."

With cautious steps they made their way upstairs. Lucas directed them to the door of their father's bedroom. The door was slightly ajar but only enough to allow a little light and sound to exit it. Voices could be heard. They were not yelling but they were arguing. They made their tentative steps to stand on either side of the door to listen. James to the left and Chalanor and Lucas to the right. James indicated with a sign to listen, holding his hand to his ear. He pointed to the room and shook his head. He hoped they understood his mind.

Let us listen but not enter the room yet.

"I cannot believe your son allowed you to stay here to rot." Alexander exalted.

"I told you my being here was my decision. But what does it matter to you?"

"It matters because you will die because of his carelessness. As will his wife and Lucas. And if I am lucky, he will too."

"You are a strange man. Why do you desire death? My understanding is you have killed many times already. Why?"

"That is simple. Because I can."

"That is no reason, man. What drives you to do this?"

"What do you care?"

"If you are going to kill me then I would like to know why? At least you could answer a simple question for me. After all no one is here to listen to your reasons. It is for my ears only and as you say, I will die."

"Very well, old man. It is because of you."

"Me? I have not known you before your arrival at Skye. You had killed long before I met you."

"Not you personally. But your kind. The aristocracy, money, families with titles and prestige. For years I have been treated as if I was not human. I was nothing. Certainly not worth your notice. You excluded me from life because my mother, one of your own, had me out of wedlock."

"So, you are a bastard."

"Do not call me that name or I will shoot you here and now." He yelled.

James looked at the other men. Now they knew he had a gun. He might have more than one.

"But you don't want to shoot me." His father continued. "You want Elspeth to suffer as you drain the life from me. Admit it."

"True. I want her to suffer, watching you suffer, then I will drain the life from her."

James fists opened and closed. He wanted to kill this beast with his bare hands. He looked at Chalanor and Lucas and shook his head. They needed to wait.

"But why Elspeth. The girl has done nothing to you. She is an innocent." Came his father's voice. He sounded tired but determined to keep him talking.

"She ignored me all her life. Except at one point when she spied on her brother and I as we were having sex with a woman on their estate. We were in a pond with a waterfall. Freddie and I were exploring our naked bodies. We were excited beyond anything we had known. The black-haired beauty came to us and we had sex. Glorious sex. Again, and again. Each in our turn. And Elspeth was in the woods watching us, lusting after my body. I could see her. She wanted me."

"She was a child, man. How could she even know what you were doing? She was intrigued about something she knew nothing about."

"Her eyes told me different. For a day after, before we left for college, I caught her looking and lusting after me. She wanted me which made me want her."

"She was embarrassed."

"No." Alexander yelled. "She wanted me. All these years I have wanted her. But her brother would not allow it. She was meant for a man of fortune, not a penniless man who had craved a position above his station in life. If Freddie had not killed himself, I would have eventually killed him myself to get her. I want her. And I am determined to have her. She is mine."

James was hot and flustered. He wanted to rush in. But he had to wait and work out where his father was and the gun. Then they could storm in and make their move.

His father continued. "She is so happy with James. She has lost her parents and her brother. A brother who disgraced her and the family. She has suffered as you have suffered. Can you not just walk away? Find someone else to torture?"

"I have. You sir."

"If I knew that you would leave Elspeth alone then I would sacrifice myself for her. But you will not give up. You will kill me and then go after her."

"You are correct. I kill because I like it. And I want her so I can have her physically. Why? Because I can. I think I will torture you by leaving you tied up as you are now. Then I will tie her up and have sex with her in front of you. You can enjoy my lust for her. I will have her begging for more before I finish with her."

"You are mad, if you think I wouldn't try to kill you for even trying to hurt my daughter-in-law."

"Then I will drive you mad, sir, for I will have her."

James reached into his coat pocket and pulled out the pistol he had brought with him. He looked at it. He looked at the men and before he could say a word Lucas made a dash for the door.

Things happened very quickly. Lucas tackled Alexander to the ground. There was a shot and Lucas slumped off Alexander, who was holding a gun, a single shot pistol. Lucas did not move. James came over to Alexander and held his single shot pistol at Alexander's head.

"I would be delighted to shoot you in the head, but you will not get off so easy. You will pay for the damage you have done. Chalanor untie my father. We need the rope to tie him up."

"What of Lucas?"

"The sooner he is restrained the quicker we can help Lucas."

Chalanor had Raeburn untied as quickly as he could. Raeburn went to Lucas to see if he was alive.

"He's alive."

Chalanor brought over the rope. He took the pistol from Alexander's hand and brought his hands behind his back and tied him up.

"Lucas!" Elspeth screamed as she came running into the room.

"Elspeth, stay back." James yelled.

———

"No." she kneeled down and helped Raeburn roll his son over. She took off the scarf she had around her head and placed it on top of the wound in Lucas' side. She had to stop the blood from flowing.

"I want you harlot. You will be mine."

James hit him in the face with his fist. Alexander slumped but did not fall. She was happy that James had punched him. If only she could do it herself.

Raeburn took the pressure off Elspeth's hands allowing her to stand. Raeburn would look after his son. She came over to position herself in front of the man who had made her life miserable. She hated him. It was hard for her to think of him in such terms as she had never truly hated anyone in her life before. But she hated this man more than she could say. She knew he was tied up. Perhaps it was the knowledge of his incarceration spurring her on.

James came over to stand next to her, still holding the gun on Alexander. With his other hand he took her hand. He looked at her and she at him. Then she returned her attention back on Alexander. She stood taller and straighter. Having James by her side gave her the courage she needed.

"I hate you, sir. I have never used the words on another human being but you sir, are an animal. You have no morals. No care or concern for the feelings of others. People despise you for what you have done and rightly so. You will never have me sir. You will go to Edinburgh and will die by hanging for all the tragic deaths at your hand. And the hand of others."

Alexander's eyes stared at her as if she were prey. But they changed as she spoke. And she rejoiced at the change.

"I now know it was you who corrupted my brother. Not he you. I do not care what your reasons were. My brother was a good person till he met you. You corrupted him. You have corrupted almost everyone who you have come across."

"Like your stupid brother-in-law. I hope he dies." He snarled.

"Lucas was not persuaded and has been telling us all, for some time now. He worked out what you were. I only regret my brother did not. And Lucas will live. I guarantee it. But you sir, will die."

She did not raise her voice. She did not yell or scream. Her words needed to be spoken so as to diminish him, so he had no power over her. For at this moment, she held the power.

"They will not charge me. They have no proof."

"Again, you display your ignorance, sir. We have many witnesses who are telling all. Including your beloved George."

"I don't believe it, you bitch."

James used the butt of the gun to hit him in the face again. "This is my wife you are speaking to. Mind your words."

She crossed her arms. "I will gladly stand up against you as will everyone here. What you did to his lordship is bad enough. No sir, you will not escape. You will hang. And may God have mercy on your soul. Because none of us will show any. You will die."

He let out a primeval scream that could have brought terror to anyone who heard it.

"Nothing can hurt me anymore. You are finished."

He lunged at her and James hit him over the head with the pistol. This time he went to the floor.

Elspeth went back to Lucas.

"Take him to the stables. He is to be chained and tied to all the posts he can be. He will not escape. As a local magistrate, I will arrange for his removal to Edinburgh with all speed." Raeburn stood before him and added. "You will die sir, even if I have to sign your death warrant myself."

"They won't listen to an old man and a woman."

She stood up and looked at him and gladly gave the last word she would utter to him. "I am a lady. I am also a valuable person. I am Elspeth. And you sir, can go to hell."

A number of men from the house who had come with Elspeth came forward and took him away. Alexander yelled and screamed. Begging to be let go. But he could not change the thoughts of anyone there. His days of persuasion had gone.

Elspeth checked on Lucas again. The blood was not flowing, and she hoped the doctor could fix any damage. She just rejoiced he was alive. Chalanor and Raeburn made a bed from a quilt and placed him upon it. Four of the servants carried him to the big house. Another ran to the doctor in the village to bring him to Lucas.

"Poor McMaster. We saw him downstairs. I had a footman stay with him. I will get his body taken to the big house."

Elspeth moved towards the door to make the order.

"How did you know?"

She turned and looked at her husband. "You."

27

WAIT FOR ME

She saw James standing at the window. She closed her eyes again. She looked at the window again. He was gone. She turned over to cuddle up to him, but he was not in bed. The sheets were cold. He had not been in bed for a while. She sat upright.

"James?"

There was no answer.

She said his name a little louder. "James?"

Still no reply. She got out of bed and went to the window. She could not believe what she was seeing, James was walking up the drive towards the gates. She looked beyond the gates to the dowager house, to see the building all lit up. So strange. Was something wrong?

She rang the bell. A few moments later Jasper knocked at the door. "Come in, Jasper. Do you know where your master has gone?"

"No madam. I thought it was he who rang for me."

"Wake Master Lucas and Chalanor for me please and ask them to come here." She placed on her dressing gown and rang the bell again.

Jasper soon came back. "Madam, neither men are in their beds."

"Now, I am worried." She walked back to the window. All the lights on. There has to be something amiss. That is why all three have gone to the dowager house.

Lottie came in. "Madam, are you well?"

"I am Lottie, but I think there is trouble afoot. Jasper, wake all the male servants. Get them to dress and meet me down in the kitchen as soon as possible. This is urgent. Lottie, help me dress."

Jasper went running as she made her way to the dressing room.

"Madam please, you are not well."

"I am well enough, but I am concerned that Raeburn is in danger and the gentlemen have gone to help him. We need to go after them and offer what help we can."

"Then madam, I will accompany you."

She stopped and looked long at Lottie. "This could be dangerous."

"Yes, it could but you will need help. And I wish to protect you if I can."

"Thank you, Lottie. Can I ask you a question?"

"Certainly, madam."

"Did you have a drink of some kind of whisky this afternoon?"

"No madam. I did spill the remains of a glass on my apron, but I washed it out."

"I could smell it. Strange. I would not normally notice something so insignificant."

"Well madam, perhaps the doctor is right, and you are with child. My mother could always tell if I had eaten food I should not have, but only when she was with child. It was if the ability to smell doubled."

"I am sure what ails me is only temporary. Whisky does not always smell as nice as it tastes."

"Very true madam."

*W*ithin five minutes she was making her way down to the kitchen. Jasper, Walker, and many of the male servants were there in the kitchen when she arrived. Lottie was by her side.

"I will be brief. James, Lucas and Chalanor have headed over to Raeburn. The lights are all on and we know at this time of night it is strange for him to still be awake. I am concerned our nemesis may be attempting to hurt your master."

"But madam, it may be nothing." Walker chipped in.

"It is true. It may be totally explainable. But I for one do not want to take the risk. Let us assume, there is danger afoot."

"Very well madam, what is it you wish us to do?"

"I force no one to help. If you fear for your life, then please return to your room." No one moved.

"Thank you, from the bottom of my heart. Now let us divide into groups of four and we will make our way to the dowager house. We must come up quietly on all sides. No one is to enter any room if you can hear talking. Wait and listen to what is being said. Only act if you believe the inhabitants are in danger. Do you understand?"

"Madam, should you not wait here?"

"Thank you, Walker, but if my husband is in danger and the others are also, I wish to do what I can to help."

She looked at all the faces looking at her and thanked her stars that she had joined this family. The servants were more than servants. They really were family. She never wanted to lose this feeling.

"Now, let us go but be as quiet as you can. We do not want to disturb anyone. Especially the gentlemen."

Mrs K added, "I will have hot drinks and food available for when you all return. Be careful everyone."

When they reached the house, all was quiet. The house still had rooms all lit up. Why? What was happening? She could not explain.

"This is not right." She whispered to Lottie.

All the groups creeped into the house from various entrances. She, Walker, Lottie, and a footman came through the back door. She stopped, seeing the body of McMaster on the floor.

"Alexander is here." She whispered. "I have no doubt. Poor McMaster."

Walker moved her behind him and took the lead. It was then they heard the gun shot.

"Stay with McMaster" she said and pointed to the footman. She, Walker, and Lottie ran to the stairs and went up.

So, you see I knew something was wrong when you were not with me. You would never leave me alone unless your father was in danger."

He was holding her in his arms. "I am sorry. I thought surrounded by the staff you would be safe."

"And I was safe. They all came when I called. They all wanted to protect me. I have never before felt so loved and honoured as I did when they rallied around me in the kitchen. Ready to act on my concern for you and Raeburn."

She went over to Raeburn who was rubbing his wrists where the ribbing action of the ropes had made marks and some of his skin raw.

"We need to have them looked at."

"I am fine, my dear. I rejoice you are safe and do not need to face the mad man tomorrow. Now I just pray Lucas will survive."

She took him in her arms and hugged him. "I am sure he will be fine. He is so brave. And he is strong and determined." She was crying. Concern for Lucas and Raeburn.

He came up behind her and hugged them both. This woman feared nothing and loved them deeply. And now they could settle down without the fear of Alexander ruining their life together.

"Please madam, allow me to escort you home. I would appreciate it if you could rest." Lottie waited for an answer.

"Thank you, Lottie." James smiled at her. He then looked at his brave and fearless wife. "Dear Elspeth, please go home and rest. Thank you for coming to our rescue and bringing the staff to help."

He then turned to speak to his father. "Father, please come to the big house and be checked by the physician. I will need your help later in the day. So have some food and rest. You can also see Lucas. He will be well."

"I will, my boy." He offered his arm to Elspeth. She exited the room with his father, followed quickly by Lottie.

"What can I do to help, sir?" Jasper whispered.

He held up his hand for silence until he heard Elspeth reach the bottom landing.

"Yes, Jasper. Gather paper and have the cart fetched. I want anything from here to be taken to Edinburgh to help convict this villain."

Jasper left the room. It was over for his love. But for him it was just beginning. He had to make sure Alexander hung from a rope until he was dead, so from this day forth the villain could never disturb his Elspeth.

Jasper came in with pen and paper in hand. Other staff came up and offered their help. Two of the footmen arranged another cart for McMaster to be taken to the icehouse at the big house. But first he and Jasper took notes, describing where the old man had been hit by the bullet. Straight through the heart and out his back. It would seem Alexander killed him at point blank. He would have been dead before he even hit the ground. He mourned the old man, and his father would miss him greatly.

The rope, gun, and chair his father had been in, had been gathered and placed in a cart. Even the scarf used by Elspeth to stop the blood flow on Lucas.

He wrote down all he could of what he could remember until Elspeth had entered. He and another footman went around the house to see what other damage had been done. After around an hour, he and Jasper had left two footmen and a few maids at the house to put things in order. And to remove the blood stains from both up and downstairs.

28

A NEW DAY

Elspeth sat in the kitchen with the other staff and Mrs K. Lottie had gone upstairs to prepare a bath for her. She smiled at all the staff and in turn they asked her questions; she answered without hesitation. They had shown great courage to have gone with her. Delia had come down to join them. Raeburn had gone to sit with Lucas, to await the doctor's decision as to how badly he had been hurt.

"I cannot believe I slept through all the excitement. I will sit with Lucas after the doctor has finished to allow Raeburn to get some rest." A look of fear crossed her face. "Do you think he will be alright? Lucas I mean?"

"I am sure he will be."

They were enjoying their cups of tea and the freshly made biscuits Mrs K was renowned for.

"That man, will he hang?" Mrs K asked.

"I think so. We have proof of him killing the girls in Skye, and Morag, and poor McMaster. I doubt he will show remorse. Even the aristocracy will not allow him to talk his way out of this. But please ask my husband. If I know James, he is gathering as much evidence as he can to put Alexander away for good."

"Yes, you are right. Now madam, off you go and clean up and then back to bed. You need to feel like yourself again as soon as could be."

"I will Mrs K."

"I will also come and check on you when I can." added Delia.

Elspeth made her way upstairs. She popped in to see Lucas. He was unconscious. The physician had performed a minor surgery, but the laudanum still had him sleeping. She made her way to her dressing room. The bath was ready, and Lottie was just laying out her linens to dry herself. She took her clothes off and slipped into the warm water. It refreshed her immediately and she wanted to know if her husband was back.

She rang for Lottie who told her that he had not yet returned. She asked Lottie to fetch the physician as soon as he was finished and to come to her.

She was seated in her bedroom; the curtains open and the dawn desperately trying to wake the day. She smiled. A new day was here. A new day brought the reign of terror, by Alexander to an end. This would be a good day to start a new chapter in her life.

Finally, the physician arrived.

"Mr McTavish, can I get you a cup of tea."

"Yes Mrs Raeburn. I could really do with one. Thank you."

She poured him a cup. Lottie had brought tea up just before the physician arrived.

"How is my brother-in-law?"

"I need to congratulate you. Your fast thinking, to stop the flow of blood, probably saved his life. He could have bled out. Please excuse my bluntness, madam. It has been a long night for us all."

"No problem, sir. And the wound?"

"He was lucky. The bullet missed any of the major organs and went clear through to the other side. I have cleaned the wound and have stitched in a few spots. He will be sore for some time. But I expect him to make a complete recovery. I have left Raeburn seated next to him for now."

"Did you examine Raeburn's wrists?"

"I have done so madam, despite Raeburn's insistence he needed no care. I have cleaned the grazed areas and have also checked he has not broken his wrist. He will be fine. His only malady is the condition of his son."

"Now sir, I wish for you to help me if you can."

"Madam. Have you been wounded?"

"No sir. It is on another matter I wish to talk to you about."

Heat crept up her neck to her cheeks.

Mr McTavish smiled. "This could be an interesting conversation."

James was sure all the evidence went down to Edinburgh immediately. He gave Jasper the job of getting it all to the magistrates. He took two other footmen with him. Once he was back at the house, he in turn would forward the men caught at the farm Alexander owned. There were only two, but they would also be sent to Edinburgh as soon as possible. The magistrates were sure to get confessions out of them. They seemed ready to talk and place all the blame at Alexander's feet.

When he reached the big house, it was already morning. He went straight to see his brother who was still asleep but well and truly alive. His father was asleep on the bed next to him. Oh, good. Delia greeted him with a hug. She was keeping watch on both men. Oh, God. So exhausting, but he had to keep going. Alexander needed to leave as soon as possible. He wanted him gone.

He went down to the kitchen where the staff made themselves

available. One of the footmen stepped up to take Jasper's place when they found out he had gone to Edinburgh with the evidence. He went upstairs to prepare a bath for him. Another footman prepared a bath for Chalanor who was also down in the kitchen waiting for him to arrive home.

"I want you to write in as much details as you can of what happened tonight. From when we left here and why, until we returned. I will wake father later this morning and have him write what Alexander did while he was alone with him and what information he was able to obtain, which can help to put him away."

"James, you need some sleep."

"I know but I will not rest till he has left. Elspeth is unwell and I need to get him out of here so she can recover."

"We have him well guarded. I have your workmen making a cart with a cage built into it so he can be escorted to Edinburgh. It is nine in the morning and you could get some more sleep while I make sure the work gets done. Then you can get your father's and anyone else's statements and head off to Edinburgh tomorrow. I will rest and go with you to Edinburgh. Then head back to Kent from there. I need and want to be with my wife."

"Of course, I will do as you suggest. Have me called at noon please Walker. Then we will do what else we can and get to Edinburgh."

He opened the door to the bedroom from his dressing room. Elspeth was asleep on the bed. He watched her for a moment. Thank God, today they would be free of the villain who had haunted their new life together. They could move on. Find peace in the home they could make.

He slipped into the bed and hoped for sleep. Elspeth's arm came over and pulled him closer.

"Sleep," she whispered, and they did.

29

———

TAKE HIM AWAY

t noon, the footman came and gently shook him awake. He slipped from the bed leaving Elspeth sleeping soundly. He wanted to talk with her but also wanted her to rest. It had been a very busy night and she had been feeling unwell as it was. He let her sleep.

He dressed and made his way to his study. There he found the statement from Chalanor, dated, and signed ready to go to the magistrates. He also had a note from him saying the cage cart was ready and then he would be ready to leave for Edinburgh. He spent the next hour writing his own statement and had sent a message for his father to come to him when he woke.

After an hour or so, Lottie came in and brought him some food and drink.

"Has your mistress stirred?"

"No sir. The physician suggested she sleep through to tomorrow morning."

"Why did the physician need to see her?" He stood ready to head upstairs to wake her if he needed to.

"Do not worry, sir. She discussed her illness with him. I believe they put it down to the excitement of the last month. He suggested sleep, good food and fresh air."

He sat again.

"It will be good if she can sleep. Can you give my wife this when she wakes? It will be good for her to sleep and be refreshed." He handed her a missive.

Lottie left and as she did, his father entered the office.

"Father. How are you?"

"I am tolerable James. Your brother is safe. Elspeth is safe and despite that fiend Alexander, I am alive."

He went to his father and hugged him. They held each other for some time.

"Father, I am so glad you are. I would have killed him with my bare hands if he had hurt you further. Can I thank you for the way you defended Elspeth? The bastard made me so angry."

"Do not think on it. I do not wish to. I wrote everything down when I got up a few hours ago. It is all here. Every utterance he made. Every confession he made and all his plans, his intentions for what he planned to do to me and Lucas and to Elspeth. He also hoped to shoot you dead by the way."

"I don't doubt it."

"But he will be gone for good. He was given bread and water this morning. I made sure of it. I told him it was more than he deserved. There is no chance of him escaping. He is chained and four men stand guard. The villagers have taken on that duty. They are so angry he killed McMaster. If he tries to escape, they will shoot him dead and have told him so."

"I understand their anger and I am sorry you have lost McMaster. I know he was a true and loyal servant and friend."

"Yes, he was." His father looked down, deep in thought.

"I want the blighter to suffer. I want him to understand what it is he has done."

"I respect your thoughts, son. But men like him do not repent.

He will see himself as the victim. It is us who have made him so. Just ask him. He needs to be…"

"Yes, Father, I agree."

"Do you wish me to accompany you to Edinburgh?"

"No thank you. I would like you to look after Elspeth and Lucas. I have servants cleaning your house. Stay here please, till I return if you please. Chalanor will accompany me and then return to Kent. He needs to go home to his wife. After all we have faced, I understand his urgency."

"I will and promise to do what I can to make sure all is well when you get back. And I may ask Myra and David Dunstan to become permanent staff at the dowager house when I return. They will be both good servants and companions."

"What a wonderful idea. I will find someone to take David's place so he can become your man."

***

Elspeth was again deep in sleep when he went up to change and get ready for bed. All was prepared. They would leave at six in the morning.

He slipped into bed and again Elspeth stirred and snuggled into his body. He wanted her. He wanted to make slow and wonderful love to her. To feel every inch of her and know she was safe in his arms.

The cart with the two prisoners from the farm had left this afternoon. They were shackled and submissive. And Alexander would be leaving in the morning. He willed himself to fall asleep while he processed more of his day. Sometime during the night, he slipped into sleep.

***

*S*he stirred and stretched. She looked around as the light streamed in through the window. She lay there and checked her body. Each part of her was relaxed and refreshed. She had a good night's sleep. Well more than a night. Obviously, she had needed the sleep and after her discussion with the doctor was looking forward to putting all the excitement from the last month away. Alexander was caught and would face the consequences of his actions. James would make sure he did not escape.

Lottie came in and seemed pleased to see her awake.

"Oh, madam, you look so much better. You have slept through. It is now eight-thirty on the Sunday morning."

"Is it really Sunday morning? My, I was tired. Has James been to bed at all?"

"Yes madam. He slept a few hours yesterday morning and was here last night. He left at around six this morning."

"He has left again?"

"Yes madam, he didn't want to wake you, but he left you this missive."

She came over to the bed after putting down the tea things and handed her the letter. She got out of the bed and went to sit at her table in front of the window.

"Thank you, Lottie. I will call for you when I am ready. And thank you Lottie for your help the other evening."

"You are most welcome, madam."

She opened the missive.

*M*y darling Els,
When you read this, I will be on my way to Edinburgh with Alexander under arrest and in a caged cart. I will accept no other way of transporting him. It was Chalanor's idea of which I am grateful. Alexander has behaved as an animal, so we need to keep him like

this to prevent his escape. Chalanor is with me and he plans to head home to Kent after our business with the magistrates.

I held you while you slept this morning. You were so tired. I hope that when I return you are feeling so much better.

I will leave here Sunday morning at six. I will travel directly to Edinburgh and hopefully with few stops. We have brought with us our carriage in which Chalanor and I will travel. We will follow the cart. There are two drivers of the cart and four men who stand guard. Two rest while the other two watch. We plan to go non-stop to Edinburgh.

Once in the capital we will take him directly to Canongate Tollbooth where he will stay until his case is heard. We expect it to be dealt with very quickly as witnesses and statements are already there. Once his sentence is given, I will hope to be home as soon as possible.

My darling, I miss you already. Stay well and rested and I will see you as soon as I can.

Yours always

James

She placed the letter down. There was a tear in her eye which she wiped away. So much had happened while she slept. But she could not help it. She had been so worn out.

She finished her tea and rang for Lottie.

Just after nine o'clock she came down to breakfast. Raeburn was there. He stood and greeted her with a hug. Then they both sat at the table.

"My dear girl, how are you feeling?"

"I am fine. Very refreshed. I am so sorry I have slept through all the subsequent events."

"Do not apologise, my dear. Under the circumstances you can be forgiven."

Heat rose from her neck and spread across her face. Surely, he just meant the horrendous time they had been through this past month.

"Did the doctor confirm your condition?"

She paused her teacup halfway to her mouth. She looked at the smile spreading across her father-in-law's face.

"My wife was sick from the first month. It is about the time you are, is it not?"

"It is not confirmed but the surgeon thinks it likely."

"I am very pleased, my dear. I will keep your secret until you are ready to tell. But please take all the time you need to rest."

"Another two weeks and I will know for sure."

"Then it will be a wonderful gift for James' return."

"Do you believe it will take him so long, before he is home?"

"Yes, my dear. And if I know James, he will want to know the man is dead, before he comes back to you."

She pondered these words. She missed her James so much when they were not together.

"How is Lucas?" she asked, changing the subject.

"He is doing well. The surgeon will return today to check his progress. He had soup last night and seemed better for it."

"I will go and sit with him a while after breakfast."

"*M*y dear sister. How are you this fine morning?"

"Lucas, you are very happy." She grinned.

"I am. Alexander will face the magistrates and then his maker. I don't wish death on any person, but he will hound us if he is not put to death for his crimes."

"Yes. But I forgive him. He has to answer to God now. Not I. I would like him to feel remorse but then I do not think it is in him. May God have mercy on his soul."

"You are more forgiving than I. He hurt me and I can live with what he did to me. He was prepared to kill my father and you. That I cannot forgive him for."

"Then dear brother, let us not talk about him again. Let us wait for news from James and then we can relax."

30

WHAT TO DO?

The next few days Elspeth spent time with Lucas and took gentle walks with her father-in-law through the park. She spent time writing letters to her uncle, Louisa, and her dressmaker. She also spent a good bit of time in the library. Walker helped her to find the items she needed.

She loved her new home and wanted to add her own touch. With Walker's help, a new bookcase was set on a wall near a desk. The bookcase would hold the archival material of the family. She had a small office, but she created a bigger one with the help of the servants. And it was across the corridor from James instead of being towards the back of the house.

Over the weeks she wrote many stories telling of the various activities of family members in years gone by. She had found her forte. That was to organise and write the family history of this Raeburn clan. She took special delight in writing about the Dutch trader and his wife. She worked either in her study or in the corner of the library where all the archive material had been placed. Once James had returned and seen what she had achieved, he would rejoice with excitement at things she had created.

"How is the research going?" Raeburn asked as he came in one afternoon.

"I can see the gaps and will do my best to fill them. I need to get some background from you and the forty years you have been lord."

"I will be happy to fill in any information. At the end of November, it will be forty years. It is also when I plan to stand down and retire from my duties. If James is willing."

"He has been training and preparing for this position. If it is your desire, I am sure it will be his."

"Then if you will, can we make plans for the change to occur?"

He went over to another bookcase and pulled down an old tome.

"This has the traditions for the ceremony. Read them. Determine what you think would be good to represent the change. I will return after lunch tomorrow and we can go through them."

She spent the rest of that day and the following morning doing just that.

James had been gone for three weeks. She had a few letters from him keeping the whole family informed of the proceedings. He reported that Chalanor had given his testimony and had returned to Kent and Louisa. October had gone. And November promised so much. The cold was wonderful, and she found it so refreshing. They even had a few days of snow.

She and Raeburn had worked out the ceremony and she hoped James would find it appropriate but with great depth to it, linking in with the family traditions.

But she wanted him home. At the end of the first week in November she received a letter from him.

. . .

*M*y dearest Els

    I wanted to be with you. We are so newly married, but I would not be happy until I knew Alexander was gone for good.

Today he was sentenced to death. I am satisfied the evidence against him gave no quarter for him to be excused. Towards the end he admitted he did the murders, and he had no regrets. I also asked the magistrates to consider he be executed sooner rather than later. Our fear was he would try to escape and cause further mayhem. They agreed so he dies on November 12th at dawn. I will stay and see it done. He screams his innocence again but is ignored. He had publicly declared his guilt.

Once the deed is done, I will travel home. I will stop overnight and should be home on the afternoon or evening of the 13th. I miss you so much my darling.

Love forever

James

"*I* am happy that he is heading home. Do you think he will be satisfied?"

"You mean knowing that Alexander will be gone for good?" questioned Raeburn.

"Yes. I do not want Alexander to dominate our thinking or our everyday life. He will be gone and can do no more harm. After all he deserves his punishment."

"And that is what we must remember. He is the guilty one. Not those who brought him to justice."

"Very true."

"And your secret? Are you…if you don't mind me asking?"

"I am. Should see a baby in the summer, at the end of May."

"My dear, I am so pleased."

"I hope James is also." She said tentatively.

"Do you doubt it?"

"No but it is unexpected."

"If I know my son, he will rejoice."

31

HOME

*H*e saw him hang until he was dead. It was not something he relished. But for his sanity and his wife's, he wished to be sure he was gone for good. Two of the magistrates, members of the aristocracy of Scotland and friends of the condemned were there to witness his demise. He looked around at the friends of Alexander, not recognising any of them. All his other friends had been arrested and faced long prison sentences.

BANG

That was a gunshot.

The pain in his shoulder increased.

What just happened? No one answered him. His vision was fading in and out. Was he on the ground? Where was Elspeth? Was she safe? He could not see her. Magistrate Desmond was staring down at him. Saying something. But he could not make out the words. He heard yelling. 'We got him. We got him.' Got who?

Then it was black, and he heard no more.

---

*W*alker came into the library.

"Ahh Walker, has James arrived home?"

She looked at Walker and knew immediately something was amiss.

"What has happened?"

"A rider has arrived, madam." He held out a missive.

She got up and took it from his hand. Suddenly, her legs gave way from underneath her.

"Madam, please sit down." Walker helped her ease into the seat.

She stared at the note that was not in her James' handwriting. She was cold.

"Fetch Raeburn and Lucas, please Walker."

Walker left in a hurry leaving the library door open. She sat there and was so cold. Was her new life at an end? Worst of all was her beloved James dead? Moments later Raeburn and Lucas came in at a run.

"What is it, Elspeth? Who is the missive from?"

"I do not know. I am afraid to open it."

"Would you like me too?"

"No thank you, Raeburn. But I waited for you so that we could hear the news together."

She opened the note and began reading it aloud, her hands shaking.

*D*ear Lady Raeburn,

Your husband has asked me to write this to you. It is to let you know that Alexander is dead. He saw it himself, as did I.

However, while he was there a supporter of Alexander pulled out a pistol and shot your husband in the shoulder. It is not a life-threatening wound, my dear madam, but he has lost a large amount of blood. And we believe some bones are broken. He has been taken to Lord Ramsey's in Charlotte street to have the bullet removed. Both of which have now occurred. He will stay there until he recovers. He cannot travel as yet but wanted you to know he was well and would travel as soon as he can.

Yours most sincerely,
Magistrate G. H. Desmond

She placed the missive in her lap.

"Raeburn, will you please accompany me to Edinburgh?"

"Certainly, my dear."

She looked into Raeburn's eyes and started to silently weep. He came and kneeled in front of her and took her into his arms. She was surrounded by her new loving family. Lucas came to stand next to her. He placed a hand on her shoulder. And his reassurance flowed through her.

"I shall stay here and write some letters. We need to find anyone else who plans to defend the mad man. I will have all those with some kind of connection with him arrested until they can prove they are part of no plot. Or we can find out this new madman acted alone."

"Thank you, Lucas."

She looked at her father-in-law, then her brother-in-law. "Please tell me when this will all end." She really had not expected an answer. She got up, left the room, and went to pack.

While getting ready Lottie wrote a note to Lord Ramsey to inform him of her and Raeburn's coming and had it sent with the rider on his return to the capital.

hey did not stop much. Food and short doses of sleep. She tried to sleep as much as she could in the carriage. Raeburn was determined to keep her healthy and well rested. At least as much as he could. A slight smile lifted her lips. So, this is where James had learned to be so caring.

After days on the road, they reached their destination. Lord Ramsey was delighted to meet her and graciously allowed her not only to stay, but also placed her in the room next to her husband's. Room was also made for Raeburn, they being good friends.

With all the comings and goings, it was a full week since her husband had been shot. She hoped he was healing.

She knocked on the door.

"Enter." she heard.

She came in.

"Els, my dearest. You should not have come. But I am so glad to see you."

She went swiftly to his bed and placed her hand on his forehead.

"Tell me you are well, my dearest James. My nerves have been on tenterhooks not knowing how you might be."

"I have been well. But I must admit the wound is sore today. The bone was not broken but has been chipped. I am truly lucky that not greater damage was done."

"May I examine it, my dear?"

"Of course."

She slowly unwrapped the wound and found most of it looking quite good. But it was inflamed here and there. She knew that honey would act as a cleanser. She rang and asked for hot water in a bowl, some wash clothes, and some honey in a dish.

She administered to his wound and rewrapped it, using new bandages which were also brought to the room.

"How is Lucas?"

"He is fighting fit. He feels both well and relieved that Alexander is gone for good. But tell me who shot you?"

"The strangest thing was no one knew him at first. But we eventually found out it was your brother's manservant."

"Please tell me it is not true?"

"It would appear he fled to Alexander after your brother killed himself. He wanted Alexander's protection. He feared he would be blamed for Lord Faraday's death. He was sure his lordship had been killed. He has since admitted it was he, who shot Lord Farraday with the arrow. He shot me in revenge for taking his protector away from him. If you see him now, I have been told he appears quite mad. Seems he does not know who he is any more let alone what he has done. Poor man."

"Well, I was not expecting you to tell me he had reappeared. Would seem he acted on his own then and not as part of a plot to get us all. But my brother's servant? I am dumbfounded."

Elspeth sat back on the bedhead next to her husband. It was a relief to be with him again. She wanted to tell him of their special news but at the moment she did not know where to start or even how to tell him. She checked his forehead to see if he had a temperature. Maybe a moment would arise so she could break it to him.

"Do not fret, my dear. We believe he will be placed in a building at the prison with other prisoners who have problems remembering who they are. When it is done the nightmare is over. He acted alone. Alexander has no more friends who have not been arrested or sentenced. He was the last."

"Are you sure?"

"Yes my dear, it has come to an end."

She cuddled up with him and cried silent tears. At last, it was over. She was sure to write to Lucas and let him know.

"How are the staff? Have they come to terms with the death of McMaster? I know it would not be easy."

"Actually, yes and no. They have mourned of course but we have been busy. We decided to re-paint the dowager house while Raeburn was in the big house. I also got some new furniture and redecorated some of the rooms for him. We also did various repairs. I wanted your father to be more comfortable than he was. I hope you don't mind?"

"Mind? I am delighted. One, you are busy and two you are confident to do it. Of course, I do not mind. Father would not let me do anything."

"I even got the two steps that squeak fixed and had new carpets laid as well. I have been extremely busy. We also redesigned rooms for the Dunstan's, and David has been training a replacement villager who shows great promise in the job. The staff have helped me move my office. I am now next to you."

"How wonderful. I like that we will be close."

She smiled and gazed into his eyes.

"I am taking interest in the family history also. Your father has helped me get all the documents you have, and I have placed them in chronological order."

"This is exciting."

"The older staff have been giving me background on various family members they knew. It has been a wonderful experience. I will show you all my work when you return home."

"All of this sounds so exciting. But what of your health? Have you recovered fully?"

"No, I have not recovered." She watched the frown cross his face.

"Oh, my dearest. What is the problem?"

"One that will rectify itself eventually. You see I am with child. We will have a baby in May."

"Elspeth? Really?"

"Yes, my dear, you will be a father. I hope you do not mind?"

"Mind? If I could jump for joy I would do so gladly." He took her gently into his arms and kissed her with passion.

"You are happy then?"

"I am beyond happy my darling, if there can be such a thing."

***

She ordered clean bandages, hot water and honey each day. She had said she was determined to make him better. After a week he was fit and ready to go home. The trip was slow. He made sure it was. In her condition, he would not let the driver take any risks. Slow and steady, he kept saying to her.

Once home there was great rejoicing. The family was all together again. Lucas was well and James would be soon. The announcement of a 'bairn' coming into the family had everyone excited. It had been some years since a babe was in the house. She had shared her news with Delia before she left for Kent. She was happy for Delia who had decided to celebrate Christmas with her reunited family. This gave Chalanor, Louisa and Lord Farraday great joy. And Arthur was quite excited too.

They prepared for the handover of the lairdship at the end of November. The preparations had gone well. They had sewn, gathered, dressed, and practiced. From the colourful costumes of purple and blue tartans, with yellow, white, and green. To the beautiful music of the bagpipes coming up the glen. James had shown tears of joy as each of the events planned were revealed. All that had been prepared had shown him the delights his wife had prepared.

After all the excitement of the day, they were finally alone in their bedroom.

"Els, you did so well to find all the little traditions of the family. Even down to the potato cakes. Mrs K must have been exalted to know that her potato cakes would hold such an honour."

"She was. In fact, I think the highlight of the day was when you took a bite of the first potato cake."

"Thank you, my love. It was a day I will long remember."

"I hope so. I know it is one I will cherish."

He placed his hand on her rounding tummy. "And having this life, part of you and me growing inside you is the greatest gift of all."

He kissed her, long and lovingly. They spent their time, the remainder of the night, making love. Something they had both missed and delighted in renewing. Their love was a blessing they both rejoiced in. And now they were Lord and Lady Raeburn proper.

EPILOGUE

"*I* am so glad we are here. Christmas on Skye will be a real treat. Your uncle had a wonderful idea." He came over to hug her as she looked out the window.

"I love looking out at the view. I can see why the family called it 'Viewfield'. And being here again has given me much peace and contentment."

"You, my love, have been content from the moment Grace Amelia was born."

"Yes, I think you are right. She inherited your beautiful auburn hair and your grey blue eyes. She is my heart's delight, next to you of course."

"I know the love we have is special and always will be. Thank you for loving me."

"You are most welcome. Thank you for waiting and coming for me. My life is complete with your hand in mine."

"Now we should make our way down to the foyer. Look who are coming up the path?" James kissed her neck.

"Let me see. Your father and Lucas are helping with the luggage. Lord Farraday, Delia and Arthur are heading up. I wonder if there is something going on there. In the rear are Louisa and Chalanor, with their beautiful son, Hudson Charles Peter John Farraday. See Lottie already has him in her arms. She loves children."

"And the very last person is your uncle with the biggest smile I have ever seen on his face."

"Nearly as big as yours, James. I love you."

"And I, Elspeth, love you. Always."

ABOUT THE AUTHOR

Joanne loves to write and she loves to travel. She is married to Andrew and lives in Central New South Wales Australia with him and their two cats Arthur and Oscar. (Meet them on Joanne's webpage) She has two grown sons and four beautiful granddaughters. Her imagination loves to take her on various trips but mainly in the area of the regency romance.

She also loves meeting new people so do drop a line to her via her website, Facebook, Instagram and Twitter.

www.JoanneAustenBrown.com

ACKNOWLEDGEMENTS

Again, we see damage being done by a certain kind of man. These men existed in this time but were not often talked about or even acknowledged. And unfortunately, some still exist.

Thanks to Hugh MacDonald, who owns Viewfield, for allowing me access to the house and grounds. And for using the house in my story. Also, for allowing me to change the date of the addition to the house, for my storyline. I loved staying there and look forward to returning.

Thanks to my critique partners and my editor. I love my cover. Thanks Danielle. And to the many readers who contacted me, hoping for Elspeth to have a story. Here is Elspeth's story. Thanks for waiting. I hope you like it.

BONUS CHAPTER FROM ALWAYS LOUISA

BOOK ONE ~ ALWAYS SERIES

Summer of 1814

"Do you know why he wants to see me in the library?" They made their way down the hallway. It was abandoned and quiet.

"No, Miss Stapleton."

"Oh, I do wish you would call me Louisa, Chalanor. After all you are Prescott's best friend. And that means we will see a lot more of each other in the coming years. I'm sure you would not want me to call you Farraday, the Viscount Lightford?" Louisa's stomach gave a jolt. Surely, she wasn't attracted to him? He was just Chalanor. She caught her breath and tried to recapture her thoughts. After all she had just become engaged to Prescott. And she loved him. Didn't she?

They continued down the corridor in quiet, the precise tapping of his boots the only noise she could distinguish. When they reached the door Chalanor stopped and turned to look at her. His stern icy blue eyes pierced her own and she shivered.

"Prescott is a lucky man to have won your heart. I hope he realises that."

"That is very nice of you to say, Chalanor. And I'm sure he does." Her stomach gave her another kick. He was very handsome. But untouchable. She dropped her gaze, smiled, and straightened her dress. His eyes would be the death of her if she continued to look into them.

Chalanor opened the door and stood aside so she could walk in. But she did not get very far. There on a rug in front of the open fire was her Prescott, almost naked making love to her best friend Bella. She didn't move. She watched with horror but also with fascination. The glow of the fire on their damp and heated bodies. She just stared at them. Then pulse speeding, heart beat pounding, heat flashed through her and she wanted to scream.

"Come away," Chalanor whispered. He took her gently by the arm.

She shook him off.

"No." Her head was buzzing. He had come to her and offered marriage after all. And she had accepted his proposal. Why was he doing this? My God, why? "Explain yourself, Prescott?" Her voice quivered as it rose. "Explain."

Prescott lifted his head and looked at her as his rush of release hit him. He began to laugh. Laugh out loud.

No. Her head was pounding. He had come to her and proposed marriage which she had accepted. Why was he doing this? Didn't he love her? My God, why?

Chalanor now had his hands on her upper arms trying to move her from the spot where she stood. But she fought him off again to no avail.

She turned her head to face him. "Leave me alone. No doubt you had a hand in this disgrace." She turned back and yelled at Prescott. "I want to know the meaning of this. Do you take me for a simpering simpleton?" She moved her hand to the right and slapped Chalanor in the chest. He did not flinch. "Get out of my way."

Chalanor dropped his arms and said nothing. But he did not leave. And he did not move. He probably wanted to enjoy her embarrassment and disgrace. Despite her churning stomach she was not only disgusted but furious. She would not swoon or cry as others might. She wanted an explanation. She would demand it.

Prescott was doing up his trousers and Bella started crying, while she looked for her clothes. She whimpered that she was sorry. "So very sorry."

"Tell me now. Why have you done this?" She was yelling but she did not care. Her pride was already wounded.

"I thought that was obvious, my dear." He continued to straighten his clothes.

"Obvious? No, it is not obvious. You could have asked her to marry you instead of me."

"Marry you? Marry her? I don't want either of you."

The sobs from Bella turned into cries of anguish. "You said you loved me, that's why I gave myself to you. You said it was me you wanted to marry. I'm ruined." She wept. Bella grabbed his arm and he pushed her to the floor. Her sobbing grew louder.

Louisa could hear voices and footsteps of others coming down the corridor. Soon everyone would know of Bella's fall and she felt sorry for her friend.

"You are nothing, either of you." Prescott continued. "I want neither of you. You are both harlots, ready to give yourself to any man. I have enjoyed both of you and now I am done."

"What nonsense is this? You're mad. I wouldn't give myself to you, ever." But her cries were useless as other people from the house party entered through the doors of the library behind her to witness the shame that lay before them. But she had not expected the performance she was now witnessing.

Prescott came to stand before her as he placed his shirt around himself.

"But I have had you. Just as you are a product of such a

dalliance. I am happy to soil your virtue, your non existing virtue." He was not looking at her but at the gathering audience. "She," he pointed at Bella, "was a dalliance, as are you." Now he pointed at her.

Bella screamed she was no dalliance but that Prescott loved her.

Louisa crossed her arms and stared at him. "You are nothing but a beast and I despise you."

"Thank you, my love." And he stormed from the room.

Louisa stood there her arms dropping to her side, unable to say anything or move from where she stood. She began to shake. Was it cold? She couldn't tell. He legs began to give way beneath her. This had to be some ridiculous dream. Her father was standing before her, looking into her eyes.

"My dear, come away."

"Father, what did he mean?"

She heard Chalanor's voice in the distance. "Take her away. Take her home. I will deal with this." She heard the tap of his boots as he left the room. The din around her closed in. She was so alone. Prescott was crazy but because he was aristocracy, they would believe him.

Her father turned her to the door and tried to get her through the crowd that had gathered. She heard comments but could not place from whose mouths they came. Their whispers penetrated her thoughts.

"Did you hear what he said? That he had had both of them."

"They are fallen women."

"They must have known he was a rake?"

"She will never be accepted into polite society ever again."

"After all she is but a bastard. That is what he said."

Louisa heard them but Prescott's comment that she was but a product of a dalliance went around and around in her head. A bastard. She looked around her. Each word, each movement and all the reactions she could see clearly. My God, what had he done? The things he said?

"Papa, what did he mean? I am no bastard? Am I?"

"Of course you aren't, my dear. Let us get you out of here." The noise of the crowd diminished as they made their way to her room.

BONUS CHAPTER FROM RACHEL'S JAUNT

BOOK ONE ~ COME WITH ME SERIES

Aberlour, Scotland 2018

"Where are you?"

"I'm on a special mountain and I am sitting on a big rock, looking around me. The mountains, the river Spey. It's all so beautiful. I don't understand why it took me so long to come back here." The sun was just beginning to light the early morning sky giving everything a silver-grey appearance. Rachael Fielding breathed in the delicious scent of freshly mown grass as the early birds were singing their wake-up song.

"Do you really think you're doing the right thing? Wait a minute, what do you mean, *your* mountain? Rachael, what have you done?"

Samantha Cooper, her PA at the firm where she was a lawyer, as well as her best friend did not sound happy.

"Relax, I said a special mountain. Besides it's not a big mountain, more like a big hill. Where I come from it's flat, remember? For me, anything bigger than an ant hill is a mountain."

"Ok… Good… I can't understand why you just can't write at your farm here in Dubbo. Countryside is countryside." Her American accent was crisp and clear. Sam had only ever lived in her hometown Warwick in Rhode Island and now in Dubbo, Australia. She had no idea what a Scottish countryside was like.

Sam continued muttering in her ear as Rachael looked down to the dark silver-grey river Spey meandering gently through the dark green bracken laden hills that hugged the river to their base. A sense of peace descended onto her.

Sam's tirade continued, about the benefits of writing in a place that was familiar and comforting. How Rachael was making a mistake at not being at her desk with her cat 'Darnit' jumping all over her keyboard. Sam had even inspired the naming of her cat when the shy grey fluff ball was found wandering around the farm. Every time Sam got cross, she would say 'darn it' instead of swearing. Rachael loved that.

Her friend questioning her sanity and restlessness was what she had expected, but she had had enough now.

"Sam, stop, please. I am asking nicely, please. Can you see me smiling?"

"Stop being sarcastic. Rachael, I'm your friend and I worry about you. You know I personally would love to rip Josh's heart out of his chest, and I know you must get on with your life. Can't you just forget him and come home?"

Rachael shifted uncomfortably on the rock. "I've been spending so much time on work and my writing that I feel like I need to stop and take stock. I need this time away. It's not just Josh. He's gone and has been for ages, and I'm glad. But he keeps trying to get back into my life. So, I want this break somewhere far away. Especially after my parents..."

"But why Scotland? Why are you running away?"

Rachael sighed, then took a deep breath. She got off the rock and wandered around the top of the hill. Trust Sam to ask the tough questions.

"I'm not running away. But I can't see him coming after me

here. He hasn't got access to my money anymore. I'm taking a break and that is exactly what I think, a break. Scotland is great and although Josh is the basis of every villain in all my books, I want to get rid of him once and for all." Rachael said. Who was she trying to convince? Sam or herself? "Please understand that I need this time, Sam. Scotland will soothe me. I can rid Josh from my books and my life completely. Don't tell him where I am, please?"

"I would never do that to you. He won't find out where you are from me."

"I'm sorry, Sam. I know you won't tell. I just need to relax. But I promise you that once I get my mojo back, I'll have some great stories for you to read. Maybe a whole new series."

She wanted to live in Scotland for a year to see if being here could bring her back the joy of writing she had lost. She had obtained the leave from her bosses but still had not told her friend of her lengthy plan.

"Scotsmen are hot I'll grant you that, but you will have to come up with something truly unique. Do you think you can come up with a series? Do you have a plot outline for the first book already? No. Don't answer that."

Rachael smiled.

"Okay Rach, go find a Scotsman who can heal that beautiful heart. I'll get off your back. But on one condition?"

"What's that?"

"Don't you dare buy a mountain!"

"Bye Sam. Look after Darnit, please?"

"No mountains. Okay?'

Rachael pressed the off on her phone and smiled. She went back to the rock and sat down, looking out over the valley and down to the village of Aberlour.

An occasional light flickered from house windows. The dawn sun was slowly rising. The River Spey was a dark silver snake like figure, in the middle of the valley. The last time she had been here, was on a trip through Scotland with her parents when she was only fifteen. She had no desire to go but once she had set foot on Scottish soil, she had fallen in love. The scenery, the people and most of all the history. Something wonderful had blossomed in her heart and never left her. And especially this little village. And now all these years later those first feelings flew back into her heart again.

She leant down and placed the phone in the pocket of her backpack. Her smile returned, as she searched over the landscape. The bird's early morning chatter and chirping was getting more intense. Watching the sky lighten had gladdened her heart. The air, crisp and clear. The grass and bracken were still green, but some areas of bracken were beginning to show hints of brown and the frosts that would come. Even in the dim light she could see it. Winter was not far away.

She lay back on the rock and looked up into the clearing night sky. Her thoughts became clearer too. Josh had to die, at least in her books, so that she could start again and perhaps find her real soul mate. She wasn't getting any younger and had already wasted too many years. Twenty-nine wasn't old but she could hear the ticking of her body clock and it was getting louder every year that passed. For the millionth time she asked herself if children were a part of her future or not. Would she remain a lawyer, even a writer? She didn't need a man. She was fine on her own, but it would be nice to have one.